Coty

Viking Warriors MC

Book Two

By:

DEBBIE HYDE

Copyright©2025 Debbie Hyde

This book is a work of fiction. Names, characters, places, and incidents are the product of the author's imagination. Any resemblance to a real person, living or dead, events, or locals is entirely coincidental.

All Rights Reserved. No part of this book may be used or reproduced in any manner whatsoever without the author's written permission except in the case of brief quotations in critical articles and reviews.

Front Cover Model: Coty Pearson
Cover Model Photographer: DJ Claxton Photography/Donya Claxton
Cover Design: Debbie Hyde
ISBN: 979-8-3494-1456-5

In this series: Ariel's story is Kacy's story.

Honoring the memory of:
Kacy Magnolia Roberson, my daughter.
June 2, 1988 – January 18, 2011
You and your bright blue eyes, wonderful smile, funny, sarcastic attitude were ripped from us. Losing you wasn't fair. It's not right. It shouldn't have happened. You're missed. Oh, so missed. It hurts. It will always hurt. My world forever changed the moment you left. Even the air doesn't feel the same. My soul is gutted. Your babies are no longer 3 and 4. They're teens now and so amazing. She's sweet and creative. He has your attitude. If I could flip our world back to right, I would in a heartbeat. I miss you, so so much.
I love you, Katie Bug. Always will.
Mom

And to:

Angel Magnolia Roberson, my granddaughter
Due to this world June 24, 2011
Entered Heaven with her mother on January 18, 2011
Oh my sweet little girl. We didn't get to meet you or hold you. But you are deeply loved. I would have loved to have heard your laugh. Sadly, the only sound you got to make in this world was through a heart monitor in an ER a month before we lost you. Nanny will see you someday sweet girl. For now, you play big and fly high until we meet. It won't be easy, but keep your mom in line for us. I love you little angel.
Nanny

Trigger Warning

This series is meant to give a voice to victims of domestic violence. The subjects here may be harder to read than my recent novels. Please don't read if you are triggered by any of the following: domestic violence, mental, physical, and verbal abuse. Loss of a loved one, grief. Fighting, death. Some scenes won't be graphically detailed. There are also things from my life in this book. Some of the things Kayla went through, so have I.

I lost my daughter and unborn granddaughter to this horrible crime. In this series, Ariel's story is Kacy's story.

This series is for every victim of Domestic Violence. Abuse is wrong, no matter the form it takes, physical, emotional, or verbal. You don't have to stay. You can go. You aren't meant to hurt like this. You are precious and should be loved, honored, and treated like the angel you are. Ariel's Angels in this series is a fictional group, but there are people to help. The Domestic Abuse Hotline number will be included below and in the back of every book in this series.

End the Silence – Stop the Violence.

National Domestic Violence Hotline
CALL 1-800-799-SAFE (7233)
CHAT www.thehotline.org
TEXT "START" to 88788

And for love is respect for youth, focusing on healthy dating relationships:
CALL 1-866-331-9474
CHAT www.loveisrespect.org
TEXT "LOVEIS" to 22522

1
Coty

Christmas was an amazing time for just about everyone in Willow Creek. My best friend officially claimed his ole' lady in front of the entire club. Jack's family, the officers, and his closest friends knew about it weeks before. Seeing my friend settling down is great. It's weird, too. I'm happy for Jack and Lily. I really am. It's just, at times, I feel like a third wheel, an outsider intruding on their happiness.

Tonight, things are a bit wild around here. The Viking Warriors MC throws a massive New Year's Eve party at the Den. Jack and I missed this celebration the last two years while we were out roaming around the country. I don't remember it being this big. From the looks of things, half of Willow Creek showed up tonight. Actually, there are people here from all over Tennessee and a few surrounding states.

Most of the Viking Warriors are here tonight, especially the older members. Our younger guys are split up between here and JB's Roadhouse in town. Nick is in the process of connecting the newest large-screen TV on the wall next to the doors for Church to one at JB's. The live feed will even go to the families at home with small children through an app Nick created. We'll ring in the New Year live with our families, brothers, and friends who couldn't be here tonight.

"Rodeo." Jack tosses an arm over my shoulders. His eyes dart around the clubhouse. Something's up. He leans close and lowers his voice. "We've got A.A."

Seriously? Tonight? Wow. Without a word, I follow my friend toward the hallway leading to his dad's office. I pause in the doorway and glance toward the bar. We have three bartenders tonight, all men. She's working at JB's tonight—more money, better tips. Nick needs to hurry up and get these monitors working. Bankz and Hendrix are at the Roadhouse. They'll watch over her. I'd just feel better having eyes on her myself.

Jack's cousin, Jay, walks by and motions for me to follow him. I give the clubhouse common room one last glance before heading down the hall. I hurry around the corner and enter the club President's office behind Jay. He and I stand on either side of the door with Jack between us. Worley Bird moves to stand behind the desk next to Mack, our President. He's also Jack's dad and Jay's uncle.

A woman with long, dark hair sits on one of the leather chairs on this side of the desk. A little boy about two years old, maybe three at the most, sits on her lap, clinging tightly to a stuffed dinosaur. Sometimes, the women we help have children. It makes things harder when relocating them. Thankfully, Nick, our computer genius, handles all of that. I don't know how the legal matters work. Nick never shares those details with us.

A light knock comes on the door. I slightly open it, already knowing who it is. Jack's mom gives me a tight smile. These meetings break her every time. Still, she insists on meeting every angel who comes through our doors.

The McLeod family started Ariel's Angels almost twelve years ago, two years after losing their daughter. Rescuing women and children from domestic violence is a noble cause. Every member of this club and several of our closest friends have pledged their lives to it.

Evelyn, or as we all call her, Nanny, walks over to Mack's desk. Her eyes stay on our angel until she's at her husband's side. Mack stands and gives her a light kiss before sitting down again.

"Hello, angel." Evelyn gives our angel the best comforting smile she can manage. Her eyes tear up, watching the scared little boy. The situations with children involved break her even more. Still, she bravely pushes forward. "Do you have a message for us?"

"Um." Our angel takes a shaky breath. "I'm supposed to ask for Jacob and say Ariel, but I don't understand it."

"That's okay, angel. We understand it." Mack gently squeezes his wife's hand. Their eyes meet for a moment. Evelyn nods, and Mack turns back to our angel. "I'm Jacob." He holds his hand out over the desk. "Do you have a file for us?"

"Oh, yes." Our angel juggles her son on her lap as she digs through the black backpack. She pulls out a sealed manila envelope and hands it to Mack.

Evelyn leans into Mack's side as he opens the envelope. They quietly read over the files. Angels come to us with medical records or police reports. Sometimes, they have both. Jack's mother turns away to wipe a tear from the corner of her eye.

Mack closes the file and folds his hands on top of it. Fighting to hold back his emotions, he lifts his head to face our angel. "Welcome to the Viking Warriors MC, Amelia. You're safe here."

"Mia." Our angel wipes a tear from her eyes, too. "Please. Just Mia."

Evelyn walks around the desk. She takes one of Mia's hands and pulls our angel to her feet. Her bruised left eye wasn't visible from where I'm standing until she stood. The evidence is there even without the reports in the envelope.

Our club Queen smiles as she blinks back tears. Her smile isn't what you'd call fake. Evelyn McLeod cares deeply about every woman and child who comes through our doors. Her smile is the best she can do to hide her pain in moments like this.

"Well, Mia. I'm Evelyn. You can call me Nanny. Everyone else does." Her laugh is a little shaky. "You and little Kash are safe here. We'll get you two settled in for the night and talk more tomorrow."

"But." Mia hugs her son tighter. Her eyes widen as she looks around at the men in the room. "We're in a motorcycle club. We can't stay here."

"Oh, don't worry about them." Evelyn casually flips her hand toward us. "They're not as scary as they look." She pauses. "Well, if they need to be, they can, but they're your protection. You and Kash won't be staying in the clubhouse. We have a safe house for you."

"Boys." Mack stands and places both palms on the desk. It's a move he makes when he's mentally fighting to find strength. These women's stories break him every time, too. "Escort Miss Holt and her son to The Haven House."

"What's The Haven House? I don't understand any of this." Mia hugs her son tightly to her chest.

Evelyn sighs and cuts her eyes at her husband before turning back to Mia. "Forgive us. We don't exactly explain things well at first. The organization helping you is called Ariel's Angels. We help women like you start over in a new place far away from…" Evelyn pauses and smiles sweetly at Kash. "From what happened. We have a house for you to stay in while we make the plans you need. It's run by women. You won't be around the clubhouse."

Yeah, we need to find a way to better explain our secret organization to our angels. These women have been through a lot. They're naturally scared and concerned about what's happening while we relocate them. Being a secret and not exactly a legal organization, we hide as many details as possible from everyone. Some women want to know everything that's happening. Others are too grateful to be getting away and don't care.

"Jack here is our son." She motions to him first. "Rodeo is his best friend, and Jay is our nephew. They'll walk you to the house. It's behind the clubhouse and hidden from view. Our daughter and a few amazing ladies are waiting to get you settled in. I'll be by later to check on you."

"Okay." Mia slides the backpack strap over her shoulder with one hand and settles her son on her other hip.

"No, ma'am. You carry Kash." Evelyn slides the backpack off and hands it to me. "Rodeo has your bag."

I nod and take the bag. Mia is probably used to doing everything herself.

"The boys are here to help. They will escort you to the house, but they won't enter unless the house mother says they're needed," Mack assures Mia. She nods and relaxes a little.

"Follow me, Miss Holt. You and Kash can get settled in and sleep peacefully tonight." Jack opens the door and steps into the hallway.

"That would be a miracle," Mia whispers as she follows him out.

"Miracles are known to happen," I say softly.

Mia closes her eyes and takes a deep breath. She nods quickly a few times but doesn't speak. I'm not so sure she believes in miracles. Once she's settled safely, she'll see.

Jay and I walk behind Mia and her son down the path behind the clubhouse. We glance around even though we know no one is out here. After escorting angels from city to city for years, you naturally watch your surroundings when an angel is present.

Jack silently leads the way. Once we clear the protective fence and step out of the tree line, Jack comes to a halt and stares at the two-story house.

Jay slaps a hand on Jack's back. "Why don't you head back and make sure Lily's okay? Rodeo and I have this."

Jack runs a hand through his hair. "Yeah. Thanks, man." He bumps fists with me as he walks by.

My eyes meet Jay's. The Haven House used to be Jack's house. A club enemy slipped past our defenses a few months ago and opened fire on the house. Jack's ole' lady, Lily, was shot. He almost lost her that night. They're staying in the guest house while a new house is being built for them further back on club property. Seeing this house messes Jack up. He hasn't set foot inside since he followed Lily out on a stretcher.

"Come on, Miss Holt. I'm sure you're tired." Jay leads the rest of the way up the path.

The front door opens as we climb the steps. The house mother steps out onto the porch. She hates being called that, by the way.

"Jay, good to see you." She gives him a hug.

Jay hugs her tightly before stepping to the side and introducing the ladies. "This is Mia and her son Kash. Mia, this is the house mother, Nina."

Nina rolls her eyes and growls. Jay hurries down the steps before she can punch him. Smart man.

"Don't worry, Miss Holt. Nina will take real good care of you and Kash." I hand Mia's backpack to Nina.

"Hi, Mia. Welcome to The Haven House." Nina reaches for Mia's hand.

Mia's eyes meet mine, looking for reassurance. I nod.

"You're safe here." I turn to Nina. "Call if you need anything."

"Sure thing, Rodeo." Nina motions for our angel to enter the house. "I promise. You really are safe here."

With a deep breath, Mia carries her son inside. The door closes behind Nina, our cue to leave. For now, our angel and her son are safe.

"Come on, man." Jay tosses an arm over my shoulders as we start down the path back to the clubhouse. "Nick's bound to have those monitors working by now. You can keep an eye on your woman."

"She's not my woman," I mumble.

"And that, brother, is your fault." Jay slaps his hand across my chest twice.

Yeah, it is my fault. Kayla isn't mine. She should have been years ago. There was a time when I thought we could have been more than friends. Somewhere along the way, things went sideways. I'm not sure what happened, though. I don't understand why she hates me now. Hopefully, I can figure it out soon. For now, I'm finding Nick. If those monitors aren't working, I'm heading to JB's.

2
Kayla

If one more guy hits on me tonight, I'm busting a bottle over his head. I'll have to use a cheap bottle of beer. There's no way I'm paying Bankz for an expensive bottle of wine or whiskey. And don't even get me started on the glassware he buys for the bar. I've seen the invoice on his desk a few times. Somebody's ripping him off.

One of the college guys pushes between two customers. He slaps his palm on the bar and smiles at me. Yeah, I see him. How could I not? He's right in front of me. The little twinkle in his eyes doesn't work on me like it has with the girls at the table next to him and his buddies.

"Hey, gorgeous." Flattery won't get him far, either. "How about another round?" He holds up the cash between two fingers.

"You know you have a server? You don't have to come up here every time." I grab four mugs and fill them with his table's choice of draft beer.

This is the fourth time he's come up here. I've seen Emily stop at his table several times. They refuse her help every time. Tipping the server can't be the issue. He leaves me twenty bucks every time. Hey, I'm not complaining about the extra cash. My car is on its last leg. All of my tips are going into a down payment fund.

"But then I wouldn't get to see your pretty face up close." His grin widens.

Yep. He's flirting with me. Nope. It's not going anywhere. The last time I fell for this took me down a dark road I never want to travel again. I swear, college guys must pass a manual for this scenario around campus. Maybe it's an initiation to get into a fancy club. Whatever *this* is, he'll do better lavishing it on the ladies sitting beside them.

I set the mugs on the bar and snatch the cash from his fingers. "Sounds like you have a personal problem."

"I do." He props his elbow on the bar and rests his chin in his hand. "I'm Blake. I've been watching you all night."

I roll my eyes as I cash out his order and get his change. He's a liar. He's been flirting with every girl who walks by his table.

"Sounds creepy." I offer him his change.

"Keep the change, love." His grin widens. "What time do you get off? I can wait for you."

Smooth. Real smooth. Not. And it's not happening. I don't deal with creepy jerks. Besides, he's not my type at all—blond wavy hair, way too friendly, and extremely flirty with every woman in the building. I happily pocket the twenty-two-dollar tip and prepare to claw Blake's eyes out. He might not be used to rejection, but oh well, it's not my problem. I don't get a chance to say anything.

"Hey, sweetheart." Bankz slides up next to me and drapes an arm over my shoulders. "College dude here giving you trouble?"

"Not anymore." I could handle college dude, but this is even better.

Jerrard Banks owns JB's Roadhouse. He wears the same outfit to work every night. Black boots, dark blue jeans, a T-shirt, those change colors. Tonight, his shirt is green. The one item he proudly wears everywhere, causing most people to avoid him, is his black leather Viking Warriors MC cut. It's enough to strike a little fear into people, Blake included. If Bankz wasn't enough, full fear joins us.

The guy sitting on the bar stool to Blake's right is lifted off the stool and deposited on the floor behind the lady sitting next to him. Kellie and

Bruce are a lovely couple. They aren't technically dating yet. I've really enjoyed talking with them for the past hour.

Hendrix doesn't sit on the empty bar stool. He leans his side against the bar, facing Blake, and glares. "The last guy who *waited until she got off* is still in a coma at St. Andrews."

Blake swallows hard. He looks back at Bankz and me. The poor guy has turned white as a sheet. I almost feel sorry for him. Almost.

"Yep." Bankz nods once. "I heard his family signed a do-not-resuscitate form last week."

"Oh, man." Hendrix looks devastated. "I really thought this one was going to pull through."

These two are insane. No one is in the hospital because of me.

"Um." Blake quickly grabs the handles of two mugs in each hand. "Sorry, miss. Forget I was here."

"Not a problem." It's a lie. He was quickly becoming one.

"Won't be one if you stay at your table," Hendrix adds.

Blake doesn't look back. When he gets to his table, one of his friends switches places with him so his back is to the bar. The guy now facing me, eyes widen as Blake tells them about his last trip to the bar. Trust me, it's his last one. They'll order through a server for the rest of the night or leave.

"You two are evil." I try to look serious and irritated with them. I can't hold it in and bust out laughing.

I freeze when I look across the bar. Emily is at Blake's table. Bankz and Hendrix growl. Whoa. That's not a good sign coming from a Viking, and two of them are doing it? Thankfully, Blake and his friends politely decline ordering anything more, and Emily moves to the next table.

"How's Emily doing tonight?" Bankz asks.

"It's not the bakery, but she's holding her own out there." I've kept my eye on her all night.

Bankz looks down at me. "Just so you know, if I hadn't known we were going to be shorthanded tonight, I wouldn't have hired her."

"You still shouldn't have," Hendrix grumbles.

"Why? Emily's great with customers. She runs the bakery without any problems. Nearly everyone here tonight knows her. She's doing great." I don't understand what the problem is here.

Bankz shakes his head. "I'm not saying she's a bad server."

"Then what are you saying?" I put my hands on my hips and glare at my boss.

"Emily's sweet. She's been a friend of the club since high school, if not longer. She belongs in a bakery." He looks across the room at Emily again. "This place isn't sweet."

"I know," I whisper. Oh, how I know.

The Roadhouse can get rowdy and rough. Hendrix is our best line of defense. He owns the gun shop and shooting range. He's also Bankz's best friend. On weekends, he's the head bouncer here.

"Just keep an eye on her." He nods once to me and again to Hendrix before joining a few club members at a table in the back corner.

Hendrix finally sits on the bar stool. He rests his forearms on the bar and watches me for a moment. "How much does she need?"

"What?" I play dumb.

He sees right through me. "Emily Powell needs money. How much? And why?"

"Sorry, big guy. If I knew those answers, I couldn't give them to you." I know, but friend code is a big deal to me. I won't break Emily's trust.

"Is she in danger?"

I pause and bite my thumbnail.

"Kayla." Hendrix's voice hardens. "Emily is a club friend. She gets club protection. Is. She. In. Danger?"

"I don't think so."

"You don't…" He growls deeper this time.

"Look." I hold both hands up. "If at any point I think she needs help, I'll let you know."

Emily needs help, but not the kind he's referring to. Well, I don't think so anyway. She gets worried a lot lately, but she hasn't sounded like she was scared. Maybe she's not telling me everything.

Hendrix glances over his shoulder at Emily. She's writing down the order for the ladies next to Blake's table. She's laughing and having a nice time. Nothing looks out of place with her.

He turns back to me. "I know you trained her for this night over the past couple of weeks." I open my mouth to deny it. He holds up a finger.

"You did. You two met almost every day after the bakery closed. Did you at least give her some tips on how to protect herself?"

I glare at him like he's an idiot. "Of course I did." I jab my finger at him. "And just so you and everyone else know, Emily already knows how to protect herself."

I love these guys. They really are idiots half the time. A woman can't hang out with a motorcycle club for most of her life and not pick up tips on protecting herself.

"She's had defensive training?" He looks hopeful.

I quickly smash it. "No, not that I know of."

"Then how can you be sure? Is it worth taking a chance on something happening to her?" He's got a good point.

I look away and lower my voice, "Jay gave her a knife."

Hendrix drops his head back and releases a long breath. "Of course he did."

Before the biggest biker in the room can pound me into the floor, Emily walks up beside him and hands me the ladies' order.

"How's it going out there?" I get to work making four martinis.

"Good. This is fun. It's frustrating at times, but fun. I think I'm getting the hang of it." She lightly laughs. "It's not cupcakes, that's for sure."

I laugh, too. "No, it's not. If anyone gives you any trouble, just let Hendrix know. He'll handle it."

She turns and smiles at the big biker. "How's bouncing tonight?"

Hendrix's eyes widen, and he chokes on air. He's about to disappear through the cracks in the floor.

"Here you go, Ronin." I hand him a bottle of water and point to the front doors. "Looks like your buddy needs help."

Whether or not he's relieved to get out of this conversation, Hendrix rushes to help Colt with a couple of guys who appear to be drunk already. They won't get in here tonight. Hendrix will pick them up and toss them into the street.

Emily looks a little heartbroken. It's odd not seeing her smile. "Was it something I said?" Her smile slowly reappears. Oh, she knows exactly what she just did.

"Girl, you know you can't say things to a biker that leaves any room for interpretation." I can't help but laugh. We all get a kick out of messing with these guys.

Emily watches the little heated argument at the front door while I finish making the martinis. As predicted, Hendrix and Colt escort the two drunk men outside.

As Emily walks away with the tray of drinks, the new TV monitor blinks to life, and the new app on all the club members' phones dings with a notification. Nick finally got the new system working. We now have a live feed to the Viking Den and vice versa.

My eyes automatically find him. I do that far too often lately. He's looking at me, too. Well, the camera. He's looking at the camera, not me. But I swear, it feels like he's looking right into my eyes. Why did Coty Michaels have to come back? Why did he have to leave in the first place?

3
Kayla

"Five!"
"Four!"
"Three!"
"Two!"
"One!"
"Happy New Year!"

The bar explodes into an uproar of shouts and whistles. And kissing. Lots of kissing. Well, everyone with dates is kissing. The single customers shout, bounce around, or take a sip of their drinks.

My eyes dart up to the TV screen. He's there, again. Who knows, maybe he never walked away. All I know is every time I looked up, Coty was there. And like every time before, it feels like he's looking right at me. Everyone at JB's spent hours hoping Nick could get the system working before midnight. The moment it blinked to life set off a tidal wave of emotions for me. I hate this feeling. I hate him. Well, no, I don't. And that's the problem. I can't handle him watching me any longer.

I slap Parker on the back and lean in close so he can hear me over the crowd. "I'll be back in a bit."

He nods as he continues to bounce to the music. The band Bankz hired tonight are local guys and well-liked in town. They've kept the crowd happy all evening. I need a break from the noise for a moment. Slipping around the lower end of the bar, I weave through the crowd to the ladies' room. I've told Bankz a million times we need an employee restroom in the back. I could get back to work faster if I didn't have to wait in line with customers just to use the restroom. I'm in no hurry tonight, though. The ten-minute wait to get inside isn't long enough.

After washing my hands, I splash some cold water on my face and pat it dry with a paper towel. Thank goodness Bankz stocks the soft towels, not those rough, brown, scratchy ones. It takes off most of my makeup, but I need to cool down.

"You okay?" The lady at the sink next to me grabs a couple of towels and steps out of the way. She's been sitting at the bar for a couple of hours. We've only talked when she needed to order a drink.

"Yeah. It's just a wild night." I follow her over to the side so the lady behind me can get to the sink.

"What's a normal night like?" She tosses her towel into the trash can.

"What?" I'm a little out of sorts tonight.

"I'm new in town. Just trying to get my bearings. It's New Year's Eve. I'm sure it's not always this crowded."

"Right." I lead the way to the door. "Weekends are steady. Weeknights are a hit or miss."

Her shoulders drop. "Sounds like most small towns."

"You must be a city girl."

"Yeah. Chicago." She lifts her eyebrows and presses her lips together.

My heart kinda hurts for her. She's going to die of boredom here. She'd fare better in Nashville than Willow Creek. Shoot, Jackson would probably be better for her. We step into the hallway as a couple of giggling college girls rush into the restroom. It must be nice to be so carefree. It's something I'll never experience again.

"If you're looking for a job, I can talk to Bankz."

JB's is shorthanded right now, even on regular days. Emily's doing great, but it's just for tonight. The way Jerrard talked earlier, he's not likely to let her wait tables again.

Coty

"Thanks, but I have a job." She stumbles a little as a guy pushes past us.

A hand wraps tightly around my upper right arm before we can get through the crowd to the main room. Fingernails dig into my skin as I'm pulled backwards down the hallway past the men's restroom door. A yelp escapes when my back hits the wall.

He leans in close, using his body to press mine against the wall. "Women like you are a disgrace."

I don't recognize his voice. How's that comforting? He's a new danger, not the one I know. My brain and senses finally snap into action.

"Let go!" I try to shove him away.

The little distance made between us is enough for his face to come into view. He probably allowed it. He's a lot stronger than I ever will be. I do know him. Well, not his name. He's one of Blake's friends. A college jock, more than likely football, from the looks of him.

"Get away from me!" I shove harder and raise my knee.

He's prepared for the move and shifts enough to block the blow. "You're trash. Can't give a good man a chance. Have to crawl in bed with dirty bikers," he snarls, actually showing his teeth.

My eyes bore into his. I hate men like this. A little rich kid looking down on everyone else. His grip on my arm tightens. My left hand slowly slides into the front pocket of my jeans. Hendrix Weapons and Range carries more than guns. This knife is specially made. It fits perfectly in my hand.

"You're the only dirty piece of trash here." The knife clears my pocket, and I easily snap the blade open.

In the blink of an eye, the jerk's face is replaced by the Viking Warriors emblem. I snap the knife closed and slide it back into my pocket. Another second or two and I would have stabbed my boss in the back. Emily and the woman who walked out of the restroom with me rush to either side of me.

"We don't treat women like this!" Bankz slams Blake's friend face-first into the opposite wall.

"Ah," he cries out.

I don't look. I'm sure there's blood somewhere.

"Oh, this one is mine." Hendrix forcefully twists the guy's arm behind his back and roughly ushers him out of the hallway.

"You okay?" Bankz carefully lifts my chin and gently turns my head side to side.

"I'm good." I take a deep breath and nod. "He didn't hit me.

"He shouldn't have touched you." Whoa. It's not often Emily Powell gets mad. This version of her is scary.

"When Hendrix is through with him, he'll think twice before touching another woman." Bankz's voice is full of anger and hate. Hurting women is the worst thing a man can do in the eyes of a Viking. "Let's get you to the bar and get a drink."

Emily and my new friend wrap their arms around me and walk me to a stool at the lower end of the bar. Parker sets a shot of whiskey in front of me. Trust me. I'm not turning this down.

"I'm Eliza, by the way," my new friend introduces herself.

"Kayla, and this is Emily." I nudge my baker friend with my left shoulder.

"Nice to officially meet you," Emily says. "Thanks for coming to get us."

Eliza's smile fades when she lifts my right arm. "He may not have hit you, but he still hurt you." She gently slides my shirt sleeve up, revealing the bruise and fingernail cuts in my skin.

Bankz growls and storms out the front door. I glance at Blake's table. Three couples are there now. Blake and his friends are nowhere to be seen. Fine by me. I never want to see them again.

"I'll grab the first aid kit." Emily hurries to the employee lounge next to Bankz's office and comes back with the kit. She sets it on the bar and hurries to a nearby table to take an order. The women were literally waving at her.

"So, which one is yours?" Eliza wipes the fingernail cuts with an alcohol wipe, causing me to hiss.

"What?"

"Which of the two bikers is yours? Both are very protective of you." She opens the tube of antibacterial cream and gently applies it to the cuts.

"Neither. Bankz and Hendrix are like brothers to me. I would never date either of them."

Eliza looks around the bar as she continues to doctor my arm. "So, where's your guy?"

I drop my head. "I don't have one."

"You should pick one," she suggests.

"No, thank you." I quickly down the second shot Parker poured.

"You can't tell me you don't want one of them." She applies the largest band-aid in the box to my arm.

"You're insane. I don't want a biker or any man." I wouldn't admit it if I did.

"Girl, you're the insane one. All I'm saying is, nearly every man I've seen tonight with those wings on his back is *hot*. You could at least have some fun with them. You don't have to marry them." Eliza closes the first aid kit.

My eyes betray me and flick to the TV monitor for the Viking Den. My heart drops a little. Coty's not there. He's been there every time I've looked up. Now, nothing.

"Ah." Eliza smiles slyly and wiggles her eyebrows. "He's not here. So, what's his name?"

"You'll see soon enough." Emily hands Parker the drink order.

"What?" I narrow my eyes and snap my head back to the monitor. He's still not there.

"Really?" Eliza's extremely intrigued.

"Absolutely." Emily nods. "Vikings are very protective." She shrugs like it's nothing. "And more than half of them are out of control, especially when it comes to their women."

"I'm nobody's woman," I remind her.

Emily looks at me like I'm crazy. She turns back to Eliza. "Just watch. Any minute now."

Eliza wiggles and rubs her hands together. "I can't wait."

They're both crazy. "You'll be waiting a long time," I inform her.

Emily and Parker laugh. My friends and coworkers are jerks.

"I belong to no one," I say each word hard and with emphasis.

Of course, the universe grabs every word and throws them like confetti. The front door bursts open with force, filling the bar with a

burst of cold air. A very pissed off Coty Michaels comes to an abrupt halt when his eyes lock with mine. For a moment, his softens.
"You were saying?" Emily smiles and walks away.

4
Coty

I was wrong. Having the live feed with the Roadhouse isn't a good thing. It hasn't helped to ease my mind at all. In fact, it's making matters worse. Now, I have to sit here and watch men talk to her. Yes, I parked myself at a table with a direct line to the camera and a perfect view of the TV monitor.

She should be bartending here at the Den tonight so that I can keep a better eye on her. I mean things. I'm not controlling. I'm really not. I just have a problem with men with bad intentions talking to her. And yes, every man on this planet other than my trusted, loyal brothers has bad intentions. College guys are near the top of the bad intentions list. The Roadhouse is packed with college guys tonight. The sight of them makes me wish I could reach through the screen and punch them in the face. Can't flirt if you have a busted nose.

"She's fine." Jack drops down into the chair next to mine and stretches one leg out. His eyes follow Lily as she walks into the kitchen.

"What?"

"You could just go to the Roadhouse."

"My job's here tonight." I put my elbow on the table and lean the side of my head against my fist. My eyes remain on the TV screen.

"Nah, man. That's an excuse." Jack takes a sip of beer and glances around the Den. "You need to go up there and tell Kayla how you feel. You're wasting time."

I motion to him with one hand. "Pot." I slap the same hand against my chest. "Kettle."

He growls and shakes his head. "Waiting isn't helping either of you."

I stare at him like the fool he is. "Took you a minute to tell Lily how you felt."

He holds up a finger. "True, but my ole' lady was an angel. I had to walk softly." He wiggles both hands. "And use *soft gloves*. Still do at times," he mumbles the last part.

I can't help but laugh. Lily informed Jack just how much she hated his soft gloves. She wasn't prepared for the full force of Jack McLeod either. We've had years of training on how to handle and care for an angel. They need love, comfort, security, and emotional support. That training bleeds over into how we treat all women. Jack's never loved a woman like he does Lily. She's his forever. He'll always treat her with a mix of his true self and with soft gloves if the situation calls for it.

My eyes drift back to the TV screen. Is Kayla my forever? Did I wait too long to see it? Do I want her so badly now because I can't have her? It's enough to drive a man insane just thinking about it.

"Tell her how you feel," he says again.

"She won't talk to me." My head falls back. Whining is not my style.

"Maybe you're not talking right." Nana, Jack's grandmother, sets a beer in front of me.

Jack leans forward, ducks his head, and tries to hide his laughter behind his hand. His laughter quickly dies when Nana sets a cup of coffee in front of him.

He looks up and narrows his eyes. "Nana?"

Nana points to the bar. Lily smiles and wiggles her fingers in a little wave. I swear she does stuff like this just to mess with Jack. Oh, he will drink that cup of coffee and enjoy every drop.

Nana places a hand on my back and raises an eyebrow. I should've known she wouldn't let it slide. She doesn't let anybody off the hook.

"Nana, I don't know how I'm talking wrong. I can say hello, and she bites my head off."

"Then talk without speaking."

It's my turn to narrow my eyes at her. "How do I talk without actually talking?"

"There are ways, Rodeo. So many ways." Nana pats me on the back twice and walks away like she just solved all my problems.

I love Nana. She's full of wisdom and offers great advice. Sometimes, well, lots of times, her advice doesn't make sense, especially when it's directed at you. Then one day, shockingly, it makes perfect sense. Sadly for me, it doesn't tonight.

"Your grandmother is crazy."

Jack's hand slaps hard against my chest. "That's my Nana."

"I know." I nod once and quickly add, "And I love her."

"What are you going to do?"

"You know how to talk without talking?" I twist the top off the beer and take a sip.

Jack looks back toward the bar at his ole' lady. He grips his chin and lazily runs a finger over his lip. After a long moment, he turns to me with a split-eating grin. "Oh, yeah. I do."

I shove him to the side. "I can't do that."

My best friend is as crazy as his grandmother. I'll never say those words out loud. But yeah, his way of talking without words would be great, really great. I'd happily do that if I could. However, I can't get close enough to Kayla to touch her, let alone kiss her, or other things. Whenever I get near her, she puts as much distance between us as possible. Speaking to her gets me yelled at or spoken to like I'm an idiot.

I look up at the TV screen again. Kayla is no longer behind the bar—just my luck. The moment I look away, she disappears. It's a busy night. She probably needed a break.

"Jack." Nick walks up with a small tablet in his hands, as usual. "We might have a problem."

Jack and I are instantly on our feet. He takes one step toward the bar and stops. Lily is sitting on a stool between Granddad and Pops, laughing. The two old-timers are founding members of the club. We glance around the Den. Nothing is out of place. It's loud. People are drinking, playing pool, or out back with the live band. We rang in the New Year a few minutes ago without any issues. It's a normal club party.

If the trouble isn't here? I snap my head toward the TV screen again. Hendrix is forcing one of the college guys out. The guy's buddies jump up and follow them. A moment later, Bankz storms out the front door. That's not good. The next movement on the screen paralyzes me. Emily and a woman I don't know help Kayla onto a barstool. Parker pours a shot for Kayla while the woman lifts her shirt sleeve. Anger explodes within me like a bomb going off. College dude is mine.

"Rodeo, wait!" Jack calls out.

Nope. Too late. I'm already running to the side parking lot. I jump into my truck and jam the key in the ignition. Nothing happens. The key doesn't fit. What in the world?

Jack opens the passenger door and climbs in. "Keep your head, man."

"No!" I try the key again. Still nothing. "Ah, come on!"

Jack dangles a set of keys in front of me. "Wrong truck, man."

Seriously? I glare at him and snatch the keys from his hand. Getting a truck almost exactly like my best friend's was a mistake. A mistake I can fix later. Right now, I need to be at the Roadhouse.

I start the engine and back out. The front gate opens before we get there. Jack salutes Ross as we pass the guardhouse. He took over five minutes after midnight. Jack's dad wants trusted patched members watching the gate during big parties.

"Whatever you do, don't wreck my truck." Jack pulls his phone out.

I glance over just long enough to catch Bankz' picture on the screen. The call rings out. He tries Hendrix next. No answer. Somebody should answer their phone. This can't be good. I press my foot harder on the gas pedal.

"You heard the part about not wrecking my truck. Right?"

"Yeah. I got it, man." Driving fast, I can handle. My temper is another thing.

We're in town in ten minutes. I pull up in front of the Roadhouse and slam on the brakes. I toss the keys to Jack and run for the door. Nobody is guarding the entrance. Bankz is slacking tonight. Hendrix is supposed to be at the door.

Coty

Ten feet inside, my eyes land on Kayla, still sitting at the bar. I come to an abrupt halt. There's a large bandage on her arm. That's more than a bruise. Anger turns to boiling rage. Nick can use the security footage to ID this guy. College dude will regret ever touching my girl.

5
Coty

Jack slaps a hand on my back, moving me forward. Kayla's eyes widen a little more with each step I take. She sits on the stool with her back against the bar. I stand less than a foot in front of her. This is dangerous territory. It's hard not to reach out and touch her. Emily's on her left, and the lady who helped earlier is sitting on her right. She can't flee like she usually does. She has nowhere to run from my presence tonight.

My eyes drop to her arm. "What happened?"

"Nothing you need to worry about. You can leave." She tries to turn her back on me.

I risk losing my arm and lay my palm against her right shoulder. "No, ma'am. Not this time. Now, what happened?"

"I don't want or need your help," she bites out. She glances over my shoulder and smiles. "Bankz and Hendrix took care of it."

Yeah, the little vixen knows just where to hit. It won't work like she hopes, though. I spin around to face my friends, my club brothers. I'm not a fool by any means. Hendrix is a big man. He'll ground me to sawdust on the floor if I pop something smart off to him. I take a deep breath and remind myself that these are my friends, my family. They've done nothing wrong. They actually did what a brother would expect of them.

"What happened?" She won't tell me, but they will.

"Kayla shot his buddy down tonight. Apparently, Landon had a problem with her *crawling in bed with dirty bikers*. His words, not mine," Bankz explains.

I twist my head to one side, then the other, popping my neck. Rich kids with daddy's money are scumbags. They believe no one can touch them. College guys just moved to number two on my bad list.

"Where's Landon now?" At least they got a name for me. Nick can find him from the security footage.

Hendrix huffs. "He *landed* himself in the Emergency Room."

"What?" Kayla gasps and covers her mouth with her hand.

Jack steps forward and switches to leader mode. "This coming back on us? Cops going to be looking for you?"

"Nope." Bankz shakes his head. "Told 'em we owned the cops around here."

"You did what?" A muscle in Jack's neck twitches.

I rub a hand across my forehead. These two are idiots sometimes. "We don't own the cops."

"They don't know that." Hendrix moves to the empty stool next to the new lady.

Jack points at Bankz. "Just in case they call the cops, what exactly did you two do?"

"It was sad, really." Hendrix takes a bottle of water from Parker. He sounds extremely disappointed. "I punched him in the face one time, and down he went. His head hit the wall, and his buddies pulled him off the ground."

"I suggested the ER. The way he staggered around, he probably has a concussion." Bankz shrugs. "That's when I told them not to bother calling the cops. We owned them."

"Great." Jack tosses his hands up and walks off, mumbling.

"You guys are insane," the new lady says. She's intrigued, not appalled.

"Who are you?" I demand.

"She's my friend." Kayla pushes against my chest. "Find your manners."

I place my hand over the spot she just touched and gently rub it. Her eyes follow the movement before snapping up to mine. She blinks a few times and quickly looks away.

My lips turn up into a slow grin. Well, well, well. Somebody doesn't hate me as much as she pretends. Good to know. I'll pack that little bit of information away for another day. It's the first sign of hope she's given me since I've been back.

"I'm Eliza." The woman holds her hand out.

I nod once. "Rodeo. Thanks for helping tonight."

I don't take her hand to be rude. It's respect. My girl is sitting right here. I won't willingly touch another woman even when she's not around. It darn sure won't happen in front of her. Yeah, I know Kayla isn't officially mine yet. However, I've made a small dent in her tough girl armor tonight. I'm not messing it up.

Bankz, on the other hand, has no problem wrapping his hand around hers. "I'm Bankz. I own the Roadhouse. That's Hendrix." He points across the room. "That's Jack."

Our future President is on the phone. He turns to look up at the TV monitor connected to the Den. Lily's on the phone, pointing at him. She keeps glancing at Kayla. We can't hear what she's saying, though. Jack needs to get back to the clubhouse. A phone call isn't calming her ole' lady down.

"You have things handled here?" I ask Bankz.

"Absolutely." Bankz gives a firm nod.

"You fine being a bartender short?" I don't care if he isn't fine with it.

"What? No." Kayla scrambles off the stool and pushes between Bankz and me. "I'm working. I'm not leaving."

Jack narrows his eyes and takes a couple of steps forward. I press my hand against his chest and shake my head. He dips his chin once before looking down at Kayla.

"You will climb your little self into my truck, or I'll toss you over my shoulder and put you there." He points to the TV screen. "Lily's trying to get a ride to town. She wants her friend. Thankfully, nobody at the

Den is stupid enough to bring her here. Now, before my ole' lady does something crazy, you're going to her."

Lily's on the screen pleading with Kayla. Her hands are folded like someone praying. She's saying please even though we still can't hear her. She's smart and resourceful. Surprisingly, she hasn't stolen someone's car to get here since everyone refused to bring her. Of course, even if she managed to steal one, Ross wouldn't let her through the gate. Lily's still healing from a collapsed lung from when she was shot a few weeks ago.

Kayla closes her eyes and takes a deep breath through her nose, lifting her shoulders. She and Emily are Lily's closest friends. Kayla would do anything for Lily. She won't risk her health. We all know Lily won't give up trying to get to her friend. Kayla opens her eyes and looks up at Lily. The two ladies smile and blow each other a kiss.

Kayla looks between Jack and me. "Fine, but somebody is making up for my lost wages for the next two hours."

"Don't worry, short stuff. You'll still get your holiday bonus." Bankz pats her on the head and goes behind the bar.

"And my tips?" Kayla looks Jack in the eye, not backing down.

"How much do you make in an hour?" Jack asks.

"$200."

"What?" Jack's eyes almost pop out of his head. "That's a lie."

"Bankz?" Kayla doesn't break eye contact with Jack.

"I'm not in it." Bankz takes the smart way out.

Jack doesn't look to me for approval. I get it. He's our future President. He has to lead, even when I don't like it. "Since it's a holiday, you'll get $100 for two hours of bartending at the Den."

"I'll lose money," Kayla snaps.

Jack takes one step forward. "You'll lose the hundred, too, if you don't take the offer. Either way, you're leaving here. Now," he says the last word hard and with authority.

Emily rushes to her side. "Take it, Kayla. You can have half of my tips."

"No." Kayla rapidly shakes her head. "I'll take Jack's offer, but you're keeping your tips."

Emily fakes a smile with tears in her eyes before hurrying to a table along the front wall. Kayla glances at Hendrix. He dips his chin slightly. If I hadn't been watching, I'd have missed it. What is that about?

Half of what's going on tonight isn't making any sense to me. The other half has my blood boiling. I don't agree with how Jack is handling this. However, I have no authority to override him. If Kayla were my ole' lady or if we were dating, things would be different.

Honestly, I believe Jack is going easy on her because he knows I care about her. His ole' lady is also Kayla's best friend. His offer isn't hurting Kayla. It's a compromise, and it actually helps her. We all know she won't make $400 in tips in two hours. Makes me wonder what she needs the money for.

"Can I set up a tip jar?" she asks.

"Only if our club President says you can." Jack motions for Kayla to walk ahead of us to the front door.

"Fine." She huffs and storms toward the door.

Jack takes one last glance up at Lily. She says *thank you*. He winks and follows Kayla.

"Here, man." Parker hands me Kayla's jacket—no bag or purse. I rarely see her with one.

At Jack's truck, I open the back passenger door for her and offer her my hand. She smacks it away.

"I don't need your help." She steps onto the running board and flops down on the seat.

Yeah, she's mad, but I don't care. I would have handled this differently if it were me. I can't complain, though. She'll be at the clubhouse for the rest of the night. Right where she belongs, under my watchful eye.

6
Kayla

The awkward silence in this truck makes me jittery. My nerves were shot from the moment the TV monitor to the Den blinked to life. Just having his eyes on me twists my emotions into knots. Now, we're in the same vehicle. Sharing the same space and air sends those emotions into overdrive.

The whole situation is insane. I'm a grown woman, not a lovesick teenage girl. Yet, here I am acting like one. I'm one step away from a Dear Diary moment. I don't even have a diary. Jack's niece, Everly, could probably give me one. She's always writing or drawing something. She's only seventeen, but she's very talented. No. I'm not stooping to asking a teenager for a diary. Geez. Just thinking about it proves how messed up my mind is.

When we get to the clubhouse, Ross opens the gate and waves us through. Jack drives around to the side parking lot. Before the truck is in park, Lily runs out the side door. Jack jumps out without turning the engine off.

He wraps his arms around her, lifting Lily off her feet. He slowly spins around with her once. "Slow down there, angel." He's so protective of her.

"I need to see her," Lily insists.

"You will after Rodeo helps her out."

I shove the door open and stick one foot out. "I can get out by myself."

Sadly for me, my childish display of independence is pointless. Coty's muscular body fills the doorway, leaving me nowhere to go except across the seat and out the other side. I glance over my shoulder. Could I make it? Nope. Not at all.

Coty quickly realizes my plan. His arm wraps around my waist and pulls me from the truck. He's close. Way too close. He hasn't been this close in years. My hands, with a mind of their own, automatically push against his chest. He doesn't budge an inch.

He leans even closer with his lips next to my ear. "I'm getting a little tired of this tough girl act."

"It's not an act," I whisper back.

Yeah, I'm an idiot. The heat from his body, even in the middle of winter, turns me to jelly. What was that about not being a teenage girl?

"It's not you. Sooner or later, you're gonna have to talk to me."

"You don't know who I am."

"Move, Rodeo." Lily squeezes between Coty and me. Thank goodness for my friend's pushiness. "You okay? No. You're not okay. Let's get you inside."

With her arm looped in mine, Lily walks me into the Viking Den. It's louder here than it was at the Roadhouse. Most of the club members are here. Only the younger members show up in town for holiday parties.

Jack catches up with us and gives Lily a quick kiss on her temple. "Angel, take Kayla to the bar so she can get to work. The guys need a break."

"What?" She spins to face him. "Jack, she just went through a horrible ordeal."

"I know," he agrees. "But she insists, very strongly in fact, that she's fine. She wants payment for her lost time at JB's. She agreed to work at the Den for two hours."

"But…"

I quickly grab her hand. I appreciate her standing up for me, but I don't want to cause her problems with Jack. "It's okay. He's right, and it's fine. I'm fine."

"You can sit at the bar with Granddad and talk with Kayla while she works. You two can have girl time after the party." Jack presses his lips to hers for a long, slow kiss, turning Lily into jelly. She'll agree to anything he says now.

"She's staying with us tonight. Right?" Lily's mind isn't in a kiss fog like I thought.

"What? With us?"

"Yes." She lifts up on her toes and kisses him.

"Let's go, lover boy." Jay walks by and shoves Jack's shoulder, pushing his lips from Lily's.

"We'll talk about it later." Jack doesn't completely give in. He doesn't say no either. "Come on, Rodeo," Jack yells over the noise.

Coty hesitates. "You two okay?"

"Oh, let me see." I place my hand to my forehead over my eyes and scan the room. I point to the far side of the room. "Yep. The bar's right there, where it's always been."

He growls and looks away for a moment. I'll take every cheap shot I can get tonight. It ticks me off that I let him get close enough to get under my skin.

"Enjoy it while you can." He motions between us with his finger. "Whatever this madness is, it's ending." He turns and follows Jack and Jay.

Lily loops her arm around mine again. "Whoa. Somebody's serious tonight, and it sounds like he's had enough."

"He's an idiot," I grumble and pull her to the bar.

Lily settles on the stool between Granddad and Pops. That gets a little confusing to new members and guests. Granddad is Jack's grandfather and the club's first President. Pops is Worley Bird, our Vice President's father. He was the club's first treasurer and a founding member. Nobody gets away with disrespecting these two men.

I go behind the bar and tap Chez on the shoulder. "Want a break, man?" He nods. "Take at least thirty."

"Thanks, Kayla." Chez grabs a beer and joins a couple of members in the backyard.

"Are you sure you're up for this?" Lily means well.

I understand why she's worried. She had an abusive ex. Tonight was nothing like what she went through. I have fears, but Blake and Landon aren't it.

"The guys wouldn't have left her alone if she weren't." Pops taps the bar. I set a beer in front of him.

"He's right." Granddad nods firmly to Lily. "Jack wouldn't have left her here unprotected if she weren't okay."

I huff. "I'm in the most protected spot in the room." I may not know who's watching over me, but one of these guys is. I point to Lily. "That is, other than where you're sitting."

"Good point." Pops lifts his beer before taking a long drink.

Granddad laughs and playfully nudges Lily's shoulder with his. "We're old, not feeble."

No truer statement has ever been said. Both men are in their early seventies. You wouldn't know unless they told you. Good genes run in both families, unlike mine.

Mack, the club President, slaps his hand on the bar in front of me. "You good?"

"Yes, sir."

"Jack says you want tips."

"I do. It would help." I add the last part to soften the sting. The last thing anyone wants to do is get snappy with Jack's father.

"Jack's paying you fifty an hour tonight. That's holiday pay. You're getting your bonus from Bankz, too." He sighs and softens a little. "No jar, but I won't stop anyone from offering."

"Thank you, Prez." It's more than I actually expected.

Mack gives Lily a one-armed hug. "Keep an eye on her, love. Make sure she earns her keep."

Lily kisses his cheek. I love how Jack's family has accepted her. "Sure thing, Dad."

Mack looks around the Den and nods, mostly to himself. He's pleased with how the members are behaving tonight. Without another word, he disappears down the hall toward his office. Two patched members guard the hall entrance. It means one thing. An angel arrived sometime this evening. Oh, man. What a tough night this has been for the Vikings.

The McLeod family becomes different people when an angel shows up. What this family does to protect women is brave and heroic. What doing so does to them breaks my heart. They try to hide it, just like Granddad is doing now. His little tell signs are noticeable to anyone who knows him. His jaw twitches, and he blinks more than normal. Their family will never admit it to anyone, and they'll never stop their cause, but when an angel shows up, it forces them to relive the worst day of their lives.

7
Kayla

After an hour, I've sent two of the bartenders on break. Jack's grandmother, Nana, grabbed Hobbs ten minutes ago and sent Devlin home. He's been here for over twelve hours. The man should have left hours ago. The party is finally winding down. Two bartenders are more than enough.

"Can I get you another drink?" I wipe down the bar in front of the man tucked away in the corner.

Whoever this man is, he doesn't talk much. He's sat in this dark corner since I've been here. No clue exactly how long he's been here. He sits bent over with his head down. His dark blue hoodie hides his face enough so that I can't get a good look at him. He hasn't spoken a word to me. He only shakes his head. The only person he talks to is Chez when he needs a drink.

"Nah. Thanks, though." He stands and pulls out his wallet. "There were four of you." He tosses four twenties on the bar and walks away.

I scoop up the cash and pour out his almost full beer before tossing it in the trash. I knew he didn't need a drink. It's best to always check, though.

"Chez, who was the man in the corner? Does he have a tab?" I glance up at the light where he was sitting. It's the only light around the bar that's out. Something about this feels off.

"No. Jack took care of his tab when he showed up two hours ago."

Wow. He was here for a long time. "Do you know who he was?"

"Nope. Just a friend of Jack's."

"Okay." This is strange, but not my problem. "He left each of us a twenty-dollar tip."

"Oh, that's sweet." He takes one of the bills. "You'll find Hobbs in the kitchen with Nana. Just give her Devlin's. She'll get it to him."

I swear. Half the men around here think women are stupid. I already know where Hobbs went. And of course, Nana will get Dev his tip. Chez is new, though. He doesn't know I work here regularly. He transferred from the Texas chapter two days ago.

"Thanks, man." No point in explaining things to him. He'll find out soon enough.

No sooner than I turn to face the kitchen door, a crash and loud cry come from the other side. Chez and I hurry through the door with Granddad, Pops, and Lily on our heels. The scene has all of us frozen for a moment.

"Why, Mom?" Harley, Jack's older sister, shouts.

Jack's mom, Nanny, holds her hands in front of her, trying to calm her daughter down. "You know, we do this every year."

"But why?" Harley whines. "It's horrible. It doesn't help."

"It helps in a way. When we lost your sister, we vowed to do this every year." Nanny takes a deep breath and fights back tears.

Harley has been lashing out for years. No one seems to be able to get through to her.

"Well, we shouldn't. It needs to stop."

Nanny slowly shakes her head. "We won't stop, not ever. It's sad and painful, but it helps us remember Ariel."

Harley laughs with tears running down her cheeks. It's heartbreaking and painful. "Remember Ariel? That's all we do. It's not like we can forget."

"The pastor and his wife are hosting the vigil this year. I know you're against it, but you can spare thirty minutes of your time to be there with us." Nanny sniffles.

"Harley, yelling at your mother isn't right," Nana says. "The vigil lets the town come together on a horrible day."

"Who can I yell at then?" Harley snaps. "Nothing's right. Nothing will ever be right. We don't need a candlelight vigil in January. We don't need memorial dinners and fundraisers in the summer and fall."

"That's enough, young lady." Granddad has been begging Mack to do something about Harley's attitude. Nothing they try helps.

"No!" Harley cries. "It's not enough. It's been fourteen years. This town doesn't care about us or Ariel. Half of them hate us. We don't need all that to remember her. I can sit right here and remember Ariel just fine without the extra mess."

The youngest daughter, Maci, bursts through the door and plants herself between her mother and older sister. "You need to stop." She jabs her finger at Harley. "You can be mad all you want, but don't you dare disrespect my mother and grandmother again. You need to lower your voice before somebody pops you in the mouth."

"Who?" Harley laughs painfully again. "You?"

"Don't think I won't," Maci snaps.

Harley goes quiet for a moment. She wobbles and steps toward Maci. I should have known she was drunk. She does this at nearly every club party. I can't watch this quietly anymore.

I move to Maci's side. "Harley, you need to calm down. You've had too much to drink. Go sleep it off and talk with your mother tomorrow."

Harley's head jerks back as though she's been slapped. She mean mugs me. Her face turns red and her hands ball into fists.

"And who are you to tell anybody what they need to do?" Harley's ready to fight.

"I'm a friend of your sister and this family." I'm a couple of years older than Maci, but we've always been friends.

Harley's laugh is hateful this time. "You're the idiot who's blaming a man who did nothing to you for the faults of another."

Shocked gasps go around the room. Wow. That didn't hurt at all. How did she know? I've kept most of my personal life quiet. Harley McLeod has become someone I don't recognize anymore. This new version is cruel and hateful. I don't want to know this Harley.

"I get that you're hurt, upset, and angry, but you don't get to hurt other people." Nanny swipes at her eyes. This is so hard for her.

"You get nothing. You're too busy remembering Ariel. It's Ariel this and Ariel that. You'll always love her more than the rest of us!" Anyone near the bar can hear Harley's screams in the other room.

Nanny gasps. She places a hand over her heart and squeezes. Maci and Lily rush to her side and wrap her in their arms. Nana cries out. Granddad rushes to her and pulls her against his chest. Chez and Dobbs don't know what to do. I'm too stunned to move. Harley cut us all deeply tonight.

The kitchen door bursts open with force and slams against the wall. It wouldn't be surprising if it cracked. Mack storms into the room. Worley Bird, Jack, and Coty follow.

Mack wraps his hand around Harley's upper arm. He shakes, trying to control his temper. "You've said and done enough. This ends now. You will never disrespect your mother and grandmother like this again. Our family will grieve forever. You can't lose a child and heal from it. This family has lost three. You may not understand our pain, and I pray you never truly know it, but you're not going to lash out at us anymore."

"You think I don't know pain." Harley tries to jerk her arm away.

"I know you're hurting, but it doesn't give you the right to hurt the rest of us." Mack doesn't let her go.

"So, you're all against me." Harley jerks harder.

"No one is against you, Harley. We love you and want to help you. Let us," Mack pleads with her.

"I don't need help!" she screams.

Mack takes a deep breath and glances over his shoulder. "Nick, is everything arranged?"

"Yes, Prez. It is." Nick slipped into the kitchen without half of us noticing.

"Ev." Mack waits for Maci to walk her mother to him. "I love you. I'll be back as soon as I can." He gently kisses her and reaches up to wipe her tears away with his thumb. "Don't cry, love. It'll work out."

"What's happening?" Harley fights to get free from her father.

"You need help. The drinking and erratic behavior have gotten way out of control. You're destroying yourself. We're not letting that happen. We're getting you some help." Mack moves Harley toward the side door without looking back. "Worley, Jack, Rodeo, let's go."

Harley leans over and locks eyes with Nick. "You did this? You found this place he's taking me to?"

"I did," Nick admits.

"I hate you! I thought you were my friend," she screams.

Mack ushers Harley out the door before she says more hateful things.

"I am. It's why I did it," Nick whispers.

Jack gives Lily a long kiss goodbye. "I'll call you as soon as I can. Kayla will stay with you."

He raises an eyebrow at me. I nod. I'll gladly stay with Lily until he returns. No one has said where they're taking Harley. From the sound of it, it's not a local rehab center. No matter what, I won't leave Lily alone.

Coty pauses when he reaches my side. "Stay close to Lily and Jack's family." I nod to him, too. "And we're talking when I get back. I'll text you from the road, Sparky," he whispers the last part next to my ear.

Why? Why did he call me that? Why do I care?

8
Kayla

I've managed to avoid Coty for over a week. The first half was easy. Coty was out of town with Jack and his father for five days. True to his word, Coty texted me several times from the road that night and every day. My replies were a sentence or less if I could manage it. Not replying wasn't an option. Jack needed him. The club needed his help with Harley. He'll never walk away from his duties for the Vikings.

No one has said where they took Harley. It's further than I expected with the guys being gone as long as they were. If Jack has told Lily where they went, she's not sharing the details. As I promised Jack, I stayed with Lily while they were gone.

Once we knew they were almost home, I left Lily with Jack's mother and disappeared. I knew Coty would show up at my apartment if I went home. He managed to crack the wall I put between us before he had to leave. He'll want more now. He said as much in his text messages. If I don't mend the crack, he'll create a doorway in no time. He's harder to resist than I let on. Eventually, I'll cave. Hopefully, it'll be on my terms and not his.

I have all kinds of nervous energy today. You can only avoid someone for so long, especially when you live in the same small town. My time of running is almost up. I can feel it.

The committee for Ariel's candlelight vigil this Saturday night is meeting today. Mondays are slow in Willow Creek. Well, it probably is everywhere. This committee isn't official, but I've been a part of it almost every year. This time of year is sad for us. The rain today just adds to the gloominess.

"Hey, Kayla. Good to see you." Angie greets me the moment I step inside the restaurant.

"It's good to see you, too." I happily hug her.

Angie will stop what she's doing to hug her favorite people. She hugs every Viking Warrior who walks through her doors. She's one of the few business owners who is a true friend to the club.

"You're the first to arrive. Follow me." Angie has two long tables pushed together in the back dining area for us. Silverware and menus are already on the table. "You want a glass of sweet tea while you wait?"

"Absolutely." She knows me well. I'd never turn down her sweet tea. That's unheard of.

I look over the lunch specials while I wait. Usually, I'm the last to arrive for just about everything. The last thing I want today is to be stuck with my back toward the door with Coty Michaels lurking around. It's best to see him coming.

Lily's the first to arrive. Surprisingly, she's alone. That's not possible. There's no way Jack let her off club property without an escort. I stand and hurry to her.

"Don't worry, Hendrix is with me, and Jack's on the way." She pushes me back to our table after a quick hug.

"What's going on?" I don't like the way she keeps looking over her shoulder.

"Nothing," she whispers, taking the seat next to mine. "Well, maybe. I don't know."

"I love you, girl, but you're going to have to explain better."

"Yeah. Yeah." She waves her hand up and down.

Is she telling me to be quiet? I'm not sure. She's acting really weird. Her behavior has me even more on edge. No message went out to club friends about a possible problem. Coty hasn't texted an update. Yes, he gives me one every day, even if it's to say things are fine at the Viking Den. The bell over the door jingles. Hendrix walks in. He walks to the front counter and settles on the stool closest to the back dining room.

"Whew. At least he listened." She sighs with relief and turns to face me.

"What's going on? You're freaking me out."

"Sorry. I got here early because I was hoping to see you before everyone else arrived." She pauses while Angie brings her a glass of sweet tea.

"Can I get you ladies anything else while you wait?" Naturally, Angie hugs Lily, too.

"No, ma'am. We'll wait for the others." Lily smiles sweetly at her.

I grab Lily's arm and pull her back to her chair when Angie walks away. "Now. Spill, girl. What happened?"

She leans close, keeping her voice low, even though no one is sitting close enough to hear us. "I don't know what's wrong. Everything's weird at the clubhouse. Things changed after New Year's Eve. The entire clubhouse is quiet. It's creepy."

"Yeah." I sigh and press my lips together. It happens every year.

She continues to talk fast. "I mean, I expected things to be different after they sent Harley away." She glances over her shoulder at Hendrix. He watches the entire restaurant, but hasn't moved. "They're scaring me. I've never seen anyone in Jack's family act like this. Even Everly is quiet. She shuts herself up in her room most of the time. I haven't seen Logan in days. Nanny moves around like a zombie. Jack's way too quiet."

"Lily." I grab her hand.

"What's happening, Kayla? I know they're upset about Harley, but nobody talks about her. Jack hasn't told me where they took her. The whole family is hurting, and I don't know how to help them."

"You can't fix this."

"What? I don't understand. Do you know what's going on?"

Of course, she doesn't understand, and I'm a horrible friend. She's only been with Jack for a few months. She knows why we're here today.

She just doesn't realize the impact of it all. I should have pulled her aside and prepared her for this.

"Look. This isn't about Harley. Well, yeah. She's probably part of it, but this happens every year. The McLeods are fine through Christmas. They celebrate it as big as they can every year. New Year's is okay, but that's where they all change. Losing Ariel destroyed them. Just knowing January eighteenth is close shuts the entire family down."

It's been like this for fourteen years. I highly doubt it'll ever change. How could it? This is something a family can't get over. There's no healing, not completely.

"Oh," Lily says softly. "I knew it was going to be a hard day for them."

"You just weren't expecting it to be *this* hard." It breaks my heart to witness their change every year.

"Yeah." She nods.

And I officially hate myself now. Lily's Jack's ole' lady. Just like the rest of the family, right before my eyes, my friend experiences the same emotional and mental shutdown as the McLeods do. You can't be friends with them and not feel their pain. They love hard, and it's forever. Death doesn't stop their love. It wraps it in grief and cripples them this time of year.

Lily leans her head over until it touches mine. I wrap an arm around her. The only thing I can do in moments like this is to comfort them silently. Talking never helps. What can you say anyway?

The bell jingles again, bringing us back to this moment. The rest of the planning committee is here. Angie wastes no time escorting them to our table. Jack and several Viking Warriors walk in. Mack is even with them today. Hendrix joins them at a large round table in the front dining area. They have a perfect view of our table. I swear, Angie set it up this way on purpose. My eyes lock with Coty's. Yep. My avoiding him has come to an end.

Lil Mama, Bankz' mother, guides Nanny into a chair near the head of the table. She takes a seat next to Jack's mother while his grandmother sits across from them.

"I thought the Pastor's wife was planning this." Nana looks around the table.

"She's supposed to," Nanny says softly, never lifting her head.

Lil Mama pulls out her phone. "Well, I'll just call her."

Nanny lays her hand over the phone. "No. Give her a little time."

"The weather is bad. She's probably just running late." I smile at Lil Mama. She's a bit irritated today. It's best not to rile the little woman up.

"We could order while we wait for her," Emily suggests.

Everyone nods in agreement. Angie was waiting at the edge of the counter for a cue from us. She hurries over to take our orders. Ten minutes after we order and have our drinks, Sherry Rhodes rushes through the front door, shaking the rain from her coat. Her youngest daughter, Finley, hurries in behind her. She's drenched and looks upset.

Ms. Rhodes begins speaking before she reaches our table. "I'm so sorry I'm late." She motions to her daughter without looking at her. "Finley had an accident. I had to go get her."

Ms. Rhodes isn't exactly a quiet-spoken woman. The entire dining room heard her. Several chairs scrape across the floor. Jack, Jay, and a few more Vikings hurry to our table.

"You okay, Finley?" Jack asks.

"Oh, she's fine." Ms. Rhodes huffs and flips her hand toward Finley.

Jay growls and steps between Finley and her mother. "What happened, Fin. Are you hurt?"

Ms. Rhodes steps around Jay. "Fin? Please don't address my daughter so kindly. I'm sure her boyfriend wouldn't appreciate it."

Jay takes a breath so deep that it lifts his shoulders. We all hear it. Mack crosses his arms in front of Ms. Rhodes, drawing her attention.

"Mother," Finley scolds. "Remember why we're here." She turns to Jay. "I'm okay. Something ran across the road in front of me. I swerved and ended up in the ditch."

Jay holds his hand out. "Where's your car? I'll tow it to the shop."

Finley drops her keys into his palm. "About halfway between here and Dades Creek." She lets her hand rest on top of Jay's and the keys. "I'm sure I blew a tire or two."

Jay nods and glances at her mother. "Okay. I got it. Glad you're not hurt. Thanks for helping my family today. Enjoy your lunch."

Jay walks across the restaurant. He lifts his hand, signaling for Cloudy to help. Cloudy Daze jumps up and follows him out the door.

"Yeah. Thanks for helping our family." Mack tilts his head.

"Of course." Ms. Rhodes sheepishly slides into the chair at the head of the table. She places her hand over Nanny's. "We're sorry for your loss. The church is honored to host Ariel's Candlelight Vigil this year."

Nanny leans back in her chair, slowly pulling her hand away from the table. "That's kind of you."

Mack stands behind his wife's chair. He leans down and kisses Nanny's cheek. "I love you. I'm across the room if you need me."

Nanny kisses the corner of his mouth. "I love you, too."

These two don't care if their affection for one another makes people uncomfortable.

Ms. Rhodes opens her mouth. Mack walks away before she speaks. The McLeods are kind to everyone until a member of their family is disrespected. The pastor's wife's little jab at Jay put her on their bad list.

"Angie," Jack calls out. "Will you get Finley a towel?" He blows Lily a kiss before joining the others in the front dining room.

"Already got it." Angie hands Finley a towel. "You poor dear. Soaking wet. I'll get you a cup of hot chocolate to warm you up."

"Thank you." Finley dries off the best she can. She sits next to Emily, across from Lily and me.

"Are you sure you're okay?" I hit a deer and totaled my car a few years ago.

"It was scary, but I'm okay." She glances at her mother. She's talking with Nana. Finley leans forward and looks between Lily, Emily, and me. "I'm really the one planning Ariel's vigil. I was hoping you three would help me."

"Absolutely," Emily assures her.

"Good. We can get together on another day without all the others," Finley suggests.

"Best idea I've heard all day." I'd rather do this without her mother present and other eyes on me. A glance across the room confirms what I feel. Coty watches me. He's going to want to talk soon. No matter how much I will that day away, it's coming.

9
Coty

The fellowship hall at Willow Creek Baptist Church is packed. Most of the town comes out for Ariel McLeod's Candlelight Vigil, no matter where it's held. In fourteen years, this is the first time this church has hosted the event. No matter how much Finley tried to bring everyone together, there's a clear divide between townsfolk and bikers tonight. They have their side of the room. We have ours.

The fellowship hall is decorated beautifully. Flameless white candles are on every table. The flower centerpieces have red and pink roses, tied with white and purple ribbons. Each color means something. Ariel's favorite color was red. The pink roses are for Baby Angel. Emily said white at funerals represents honor, peace, and innocence. This is a memorial service, yet it always feels like a funeral to me. The purple ribbon is for domestic violence. Nanny refuses to use purple when they honor Ariel's birthday in June.

Kayla, Lily, Emily, and Finley did a great job putting this together. A somber feeling settled over the room when Jack's family walked in. The candlelight vigil does bring people together to remember Ariel. From what I'm witnessing tonight, Harley was right. More than half of these people are here for show, not because they care about the McLeods. Reporters from the local paper, radio station, and news channel are here. If you ask me, it's why most of these people showed up tonight. I'll never say that to Jack or his family, especially not to Nanny.

Pastor Rhodes and his family stand in front of the room on a small stage. Jack and his family stand next to a table with special candles that Finley ordered. One is red with Ariel's name on the holder. The other is light pink with Angel's name on it. It's a really sweet gesture. Jack's parents will treasure those.

Nanny holds the lighter. Her hand visibly shakes, even from the back of the room. Mack covers her hand with his to help steady her. After a prayer from Pastor Rhodes, Jack's parents light the candles. The only member of their family who isn't here is Harley. She's getting the help she needs. However, it feels wrong without her.

I'm leaning against the back wall, near the exit door, watching everything. Movement to my right catches my eye. Kayla slips outside. A quick glance around the room assures me everything's fine. It's doubtful anything bad would happen at a church. Well, as long as we keep Jay away from the Pastor's son, Matthew, things should be fine. No one knows what happened between those two. Hendrix is on Jay duty tonight. I kind of feel bad for the big guy. He and Jay are about the same size. Hendrix is a little bigger, but Jay isn't easy to take down, especially when he's angry.

I wouldn't abandon my post if everything weren't okay. Dipping my chin once at Bankz, I slowly slip outside. Kayla's nowhere in sight. A weird feeling rolls down my spine. Where is she? I hurry around the corner of the fellowship hall and find her leaning against the building. I get it. The room is stuffy and full of tension. Fresh air can clear your mind. She's safe. My nerves and emotions still need a moment to settle down, though.

"You okay?" I stand in front of her. She's close enough to touch, but I don't.

"Yeah. These things just get to me."

I know exactly how she feels. It takes the entire club to hold Jack's family together this month. It'll be another couple of weeks before they start coming out of the darkness that swallows them up in January.

"You need anything?"

"Yeah. I need your help."

For a moment, I'm stunned into silence. Those are words I never expected from her lips. They had to be hard for her to say. I'll take it, though. My hope rises a little. Okay, a lot.

"Anything. Name it." I'd rope the moon if she asked me to.

"They're lighting the candles." Her aqua colored eyes meet mine. I nod. "In about thirty minutes, I need you to help me get our people to the Den." She glances away nervously.

Our people. Those words give me more hope. She's always belonged within the club, no matter how much her father hates it. But wait. What she's asking for doesn't make sense.

"You know these things last for hours. Why would we need to get everyone out of here?"

She drops her eyes to the ground. "Yeah, but this one won't."

Every nerve in my body feels like needles piercing my skin. That's not right. Nearly every member of the club and their families are inside this building.

"What's going on, Lala? What are you not telling me?"

Her lips slightly part as her eyes snap back to mine. I didn't mean to let Lala slip out. It's what happens when I'm comfortable around her. My youngest sister, Mary, has always called her Lala. Mary was a late surprise for my family. She's the same age as Everly. They're best friends. She's inside with Everly right now. My sister, Ember, is too. She's Maci's best friend. They're roommates at college. Mary couldn't say Kayla when she was little. Her name came out as Lala. I don't get it. It doesn't rhyme, but it stuck with my family. My parents still call her Lala at times. I want to be nostalgic and explore this. I can't. Everyone we love is inside.

I gently place my hands on her upper arms. "I need to know."

"Um." She looks from side to side. No one's out here but us. "Finley's father told her this had to wrap up thirty minutes after the candle lighting."

"Why?"

"I don't really know." She shrugs. "Something about getting things cleaned up for church in the morning."

Right. I step back, releasing her. I run my hand over my mouth and down my chin. They don't have church service in the fellowship hall. We're bikers. We're not easily accepted around here. Harley was right about a lot of things. It doesn't matter at the moment. We need to get our people out of here quickly. It's more than I can handle alone.

"Okay. I'll get Worley Bird to help." Our VP is very skilled at moving our guys along. "We'll round up a few more members and send everyone home."

"No." She steps forward and grabs my hand. I don't point it out. "Finley felt bad. She really tried to get her father to listen. She told him Jack's family needed more time. Finley ordered extra of everything. She arranged a longer vigil at the clubhouse. So, send everyone to the Den."

I raise an eyebrow. "Finley Rhodes was at the Den?"

"She'd be better off there." Kayla huffs and crosses her arms. "But no. She wasn't there. Emily's setting everything up now. Just get the Vikings out of here as calmly as you can." She nudges me toward the back of the building.

I pause and spin around. "Emily Powell is at the Den, alone with the prospects?"

"No." She tosses her hands up like I'm an idiot. "Nick's there. He sent the two prospects to the guardhouse. The ladies from the Haven House are helping her."

"That's not a good idea." This night has gone all kinds of ways wrong.

"Why?" She crosses her arms again, challenging me. "Because Jack won't tell Lily that Nina is here?"

"Uh."

She jabs her finger at me. "You need to tell your friend to tell his ole' lady that her friend is here and soon, or I will."

"Please don't. Let Jack do that."

"Fine." She narrows her eyes. "But he needs to do it real soon."

That's one thing she and I agree on. I've been telling Jack for over a month to tell Lily that Nina is in Willow Creek and on club property. I understand his argument, too. There's more at stake than Lily knowing her friend is here.

Plus, this time of year flips Jack out. Once New Year's Day hits, the day of Ariel's death looms over his family like a dark cloud. A cloud isn't the right word. Darkness swallows up the McLeod family. It surrounds the rest of us who try to hold them together. We'll deal with telling Lily about Nina on another day. I need to find Worley and fast.

"Come on." I motion toward the back door. I'm not leaving her out here alone. There's no telling how everyone will take being rushed out of here.

Thankfully, she doesn't fight me. "Okay. I'll get Lil Mama and Ross' wife to help with the families."

That's not a bad idea. Quick thinking on her part. I hold the door open and wait for her to enter ahead of me. Kayla goes straight to Lil Mama. With her hand up to cover her mouth, Kayla tells her what's happening. Bankz' mother's eyes widen, and her mouth falls open. She snaps it shut and turns three shades of red. Okay. That might not have been a good idea after all. I can't help Kayla right now. I have my own mission. It takes a moment to find Worley, Bankz, and Hendrix. As quickly as possible, I weave through the tables to where they're standing against the wall. We quickly pass the word to as many members as we can. Sadly, I don't reach Jack's family in time.

Nanny and Mack have laid the lighter on the table. They stand there, watching the candles burn in memory of their daughter and granddaughter. Mack has his arms around his wife. Nanny cries against his shoulder. Jack, Lily, Jay, and Maci hold Everly and Logan. Granddad has Nana wrapped in his arms. This is the saddest part of these ceremonies. This family has experienced so much loss. Again, I can agree with Harley. I'm not sure how much these ceremonies help.

Pastor Rhodes approaches the microphone with his son at his side before I can reach Jack. My eyes lock with Matthew's as I move closer to the McLeods. There's no love lost with that man. He was never the good kid he pretends to be. Well, maybe he's straightened up. Don't know. Don't care right now. The disgust in Matthew's eyes confirms he knows what his dad is about to do, and he's not going to try to stop him. That makes him scum in my book, Pastor's son or not. Pastor Rhodes taps the microphone. Everyone pauses and glances up.

"Thank you all for coming out tonight to help us remember Ariel McLeod. It's a horrible day, indeed." Pastor Rhodes slightly shakes his head. "She was a lovely young lady who was taken from us way too soon. Keep her children, parents, and family in your prayers. If you brought food, thank you. You may collect your dishes and head on home. We'll see you at service in the morning."

The people on the other side of the room begin gathering their things and cleaning up. Kayla and Lil Mama managed to inform most of our side. They gather their things, too. Jack's family looks lost. They're definitely confused.

Finley rushes to her father as he walks down the steps. "Daddy, please don't do this. They need more time."

"We've had this conversation already, Finley." He gently pats her arm. "You did a great job tonight."

Matthew douses the candle flames. Yep. He was in on it. He hasn't changed a bit. Worley and I finally make it to Jack and his father.

"What's going on?" Nanny looks around the room.

"You can have the candles. They were made special for your family." Matthew removes Ariel's candle and holder from the pedestal.

Finley rushes over and swats her brother's hands away. "Don't touch them. I got it."

"Of course, you do," he mumbles. One look at Jack and Jay has him hurrying to catch up with his father.

Finley gently wraps a hand towel around the candles and offers them to Nanny and Nana. "I'm so sorry. I tried to change his mind."

"He's kicking us out?" Nanny blinks several times.

"I'm so sorry," Finley apologizes again. "I really thought he'd change his mind."

Nanny's eyes lock with the Pastor's wife's. "Are you serious?"

Sherry Rhodes clasps her hands together. "Evelyn, it was a lovely ceremony. Finley did an amazing job organizing this. We're so sorry for your loss. We hope you light the candles often for Ariel."

Mack gently places a hand on his wife's shoulder. "We need to go, love."

What's happening hits Nanny like a tidal wave, and the hurricane she is unleashes. "Are you insane?" She yells. She draws back and throws the candle at Mrs. Rhodes, hitting her on the shoulder. "Keep your blasted candle! I don't want anything from you! You feed us, say a few nice words, let us light candles, and then throw us out? You're fake! You don't care about our family! You never liked Ariel! I don't *ever* want to hear you say her name again!"

"Ev, let's go, love. Everyone's going to the Den." Mack tries to calm her down.

"No!" Nanny pushes away from him, her sights set on the Pastor and his wife. "You're horrible people. Don't ever speak to us again. My child and granddaughter were murdered! And you have the gall to play nice and pretend to care? You don't." She shakes her head and keeps trying to push Mack's hands away. "It's all for show. You're only doing it because cameras and reporters are here."

"Jacob, you need to take your wife and leave." Pastor Rhodes wraps an arm around his wife and lifts his chin. He's not this brave. Nanny's right. It's only for the cameras. And yes, they're recording everything.

"You're absolutely right." Mack scoops Nanny up and carries her out the door as she continues to scream. The rest of their family follows.

Finley wipes tears from her cheeks. "I'm so so sorry, Coty."

"Not your fault, Fin."

"Don't let them hate me," she whispers.

"The Vikings and McLeods will never hate you," I assure her. "You're not like the rest of your family." She's not.

Finley is the only member of her family who knows how to love unconditionally. Half this town could take lessons from her on kindness. After ensuring every Viking is out of the fellowship hall, I nod to Finley and leave.

10
Coty

Is it possible to have a quiet uproar? Maybe quiet chaos is a better word. I don't know, but the atmosphere at the Den is all out of sorts tonight. It's not half as loud as it usually is here on the weekend. It's the reason I consider the word quiet. The Den is nowhere near as quiet as the church was. There's just an odd kind of energy flowing through the clubhouse tonight. No one here thinks twice or cuts their eyes because the younger kids are restless. Most are too young to understand what today means.

Every adult knows what happened tonight. Everyone's outraged. Thankfully, all the ole' ladies jumped in and took over handling the candlelight vigil. Hundreds of calls have come in apologizing for what happened. A larger television news channel in Nashville picked up the local station's video and plastered it on all of their social media sites. The entire state of Tennessee and half the country will know what happened by morning.

Sadly, the clip going around is where Jack's mother threw the candle at the Pastor's wife. The viewers are split on who they sympathize with. The story of Ariel's death has sprung to life again. Nick tries to keep as much as possible off the internet so Jack's family won't see it. He had to call in help from his fellow computer geeks. They're efforts are pointless tonight.

"Prez called a meeting." Worley slaps me on the back as he walks by. He disappears down the hallway and not into Church. Our Church is nothing like the one we just left.

"You good here?" Kayla's behind the bar. I want to keep her in my sight, but duty calls.

"Yeah. I'll help Lil Mama and Deanna watch things out here." Any other night, she'd have something snappy to say. Deanna is Ross's wife. She steps in every time the club needs her.

"Thanks. Keep an eye on Emily, too." I motion with my head to where Emily sits at the bar next to Pops. It's off not seeing Granddad with him.

Kayla huffs out a breath. "All y'all need to stop worrying about Emily. She belongs here."

She's not wrong. Emily has been a friend of the club since she was a teenager. Her parents are another story. They disowned her right out of high school because she repeatedly stood up for club members. I pause in the doorway and glance over my shoulder. Kayla's father and brother hate us, too. Makes me wonder about some things.

"Let's go, Rodeo." Bankz hurries past me.

"Feel your pain, man." Hendrix is right behind him—no clue what he means.

"She's safe. No one here will touch her," Jay assures me.

That's true. Only club members and our local friends are here tonight. This is the safest atmosphere Kayla and Emily could be in. Knowing it doesn't make leaving her easy, though. Jack's family needs me, so I turn and follow Jay to Mack's office.

Worley's waiting for us at the door. His lips press together to the point they almost turn white. His eyes narrow as he glances up and down the hall. We all know enough not to speak. The big guy is beyond pissed. Nick's at the desk on his laptop. He jumps to his feet when Mack storms through the door.

"How bad?" Mack asks Nick before he reaches the desk.

Nick quickly slides his computer to the side of the desk and pulls up a straightback chair. "Sorry, Prez. It's going to be a rough few days. We're taking down as much as we can as fast as we can." He sighs and shakes his head. "There's not a lot we can do with the news channels without a court order."

Worley moves behind Mack's chair and places his hand on his shoulder. "What do you need?"

Mack runs a hand through his hair. His eyes bounce around, not settling on anything or anyone. "My daughter back. My wife's mind clear. Her pain gone." He tosses his hands up. "I don't know anymore."

Jack sucks a breath in through his nose and swipes the back of his hand across it. Jay and I move to his side. My friend is tough. Seeing his mom fall to pieces brings us all to our knees.

"What's our next step?" Jack asks.

Next steps are how we move forward. It usually involves an angel. Those steps aren't so clear when our families are involved. They don't help with our sanity, for darn sure. Our sanity is completely gone in moments like this. The room stays quiet for a long moment.

"You still want Church tomorrow?" Nick breaks the silence.

Mack leans back and nods. "Yeah. Move it to two. I wanna make sure the kids, Ev, and the rest of my family are okay before I leave them."

"Where's everyone staying tonight. We'll set up guards outside the houses," Hendrix offers.

Mack looks across the desk at Jack. "My house." He leaves no room for defiance.

"Yeah, Dad. Lily and I'll be there." Jack's learning to trust his father's judgement, whether he agrees with him or not.

"Mom's helping at the Haven House tonight. I'll be between there and your house," Jay says.

Mack looks up at Worley. They have a silent conversation for a moment. They've been best friends practically from birth, like Jack and me. We've seen them do this hundreds of times. Still, it creeps me out. Worley gives a firm nod and takes a step back.

Mack meets Jack's eyes again. "Nina Lowe has decided to stay in Willow Creek and remain the Haven House mother. She doesn't want to be separated from her family again. You need to tell Lily she's here."

Jack leans forward. "Is that a good idea? Her ex still hasn't been caught."

Nina is one of the first angels the Vikings rescued. Her abusive ex went into hiding before the cops or we could find him. He disappeared just as we had helped Nina do for twelve years.

"Good or not, she's refusing to leave. If we don't protect her, she'll find a place in town, and that's worse." Jay looks from Jack to his uncle. "And that's not all." Mack nods for him to continue. "Mom told me a few minutes ago that Mia Holt decided to stay in Willow Creek, too."

Nick flips open a notebook on the desk and jots down the information. "I'll work on getting both ladies and Miss Holt's son new IDs."

"There's not much more we can do tonight, and I need to get back to my family." Mack stands. "Nick, you and your brother's team keep monitoring the internet. Do what you can. We'll handle the fallout later. Get those IDs asap."

"I'm on it, Prez." Nick's gaze snaps back to his computer. His fingers move rapidly over the keyboard.

"Rodeo." Mack clamps a hand on my shoulder. "You, Hendrix, and Bankz make sure everyone gets home safe. Ember and Mary are at my house tonight."

"Will do, Prez." I figured my sisters would stay with Maci and Everly tonight.

Hendrix and Bankz nod, accepting their assignment. They leave to make rounds around the Den. No one will act up tonight. This day weakens the entire club. With Hendrix around, they'd think twice about acting up on a regular day. The three of us will escort the families home in case there's trouble. It's doubtful anyone from the church would do anything. With all the news footage and social media posts, our enemies might. It's best not to take chances tonight.

"Worley's in charge tonight." Mack leaves through the side door we use for the angels. Jay follows him.

Jack walks with me to the Den. I don't push him to speak. I let him look around the room until he's satisfied that things are okay. Well, as okay as they can be. The tables have the same candles and flowers as the church. Pictures of Ariel, some when she was a kid and some with

Logan and Everly, sit on each table. Memories that pull on all of us, especially Jack's family. I wish I could take away his pain.

After another long moment, Jack takes a shaky breath. "Kayla was going to stay with us tonight. Since we're at my parents' now, see if she and Emily will stay together tonight. Put a guard on them."

"Don't worry. I got this, " I assure him. "You go take care of your family."

My friend disappears down the hall, back to the side exit. He needn't worry, I'll gladly help Worley watch over the club tonight. I glance toward the bar, to Kayla. Her eyes meet mine. There's no reason for either of us to smile, not that she smiles at me often anymore. No guards have to be assigned to her and Emily tonight. That position is mine.

11
Kayla

"You want coffee, tea, beer, or something stronger?" Emily tosses her purse in a chair and goes straight to the kitchen.

I could go for something stronger. Maybe a whole case of it. This day is bad enough as it is. What happened at the church tonight was horrifying. I stopped looking at my social media accounts hours ago. Getting plastered won't help. I'm actually surprised she has something stronger.

"Beer or coffee is fine with me." I set my overnight bag on the floor next to the couch. She and I have one-bedroom apartments. Her couch is comfy, mine isn't.

"We can have both." She grabs a couple of beers from the fridge. Sure enough, a bottle of whiskey sits on the counter. Whoa. Way to go Emily.

I take one of the beers and twist the top off. "Thanks for letting me stay here tonight."

"Anytime, girl." She takes a sip of hers. "We should do this more often. My lease ends in August. Might as well enjoy it while I can."

"Wish my place was bigger. We could be roommates." I haven't had a roommate since college. It's why I swore I'd never do it again. I'd make an exception for Emily, though.

"Same." She taps her bottle against mine and takes another sip. "Oh." She quickly pulls an envelope from one of the kitchen drawers. "Here you go."

I flip the envelope over a few times. It's a plain white sealed envelope with my name written on it. I open it and pull out a hundred-dollar bill. "What's this?"

"It's the hundred-dollar tip you slipped into my apron on New Year's Eve." She gets a fruit tray from the fridge and sets it on the table. "It's nice of you, but the more I thought about it, I just couldn't keep it."

"Uh, Emily." I lay the envelope on the table and push it to her. "I didn't give you this."

I mentally kick myself. If I had thought to slip a few bucks into her apron that night, I would have. She sure needs it. Not a hundred, though. That's too obvious.

"Who else would do it?" She looks at the money as if it holds some secret. Well, it does, but she won't find it written on there.

Good question. I wish I had the answer for her.

"You're beautiful. Maybe one of those college guys fell in love with you that night." I grin and playfully wiggle my eyebrows. "He could come back looking for you."

"Oh, please. No, not that. It was bad enough when we thought the flower deliveries at the bakery were from a secret admirer." She sighs and looks away. "That would have been a better option, though."

The heavy, gloomy feeling from earlier tonight settles over us again.

At first, Jack believed Emily or one of her employees had a secret admirer. Those flowers were from Lily's abusive ex. Each carried a message. The last one warned of Lily's death. As beautiful as flowers are, they can be creepy, too. A knock at the door startles us from our thoughts.

"Were you expecting someone?"

I shake my head. Emily opens the kitchen drawer again and pulls out the knife Jay gave her. My eyes widen when she flips it open with ease.

Whoa. Just how many knife lessons did Jay give her? Maybe I should talk to him if Emily is this comfortable using a knife.

She silently moves through her small living room to the front door. She checks the peephole and glares at me over her shoulder. What? Why am I in trouble?

Emily closes the knife, slips it into her pocket, and opens the door. "Hey, Rodeo. Come on in."

Great. I should have known. I speak kindly once, and now he's everywhere.

"Emily." His eyes land on me as he steps inside.

"Wonder what brought you by?" She wiggles her eyebrows at me this time. She's insane.

"Just making sure you two are good for the night. Need anything?"

"I need a shower. Kayla can get you a beer or cup of coffee." Emily slips off to her room. She's not smooth about this at all.

Coty and I stand in the living room, maybe four feet apart. Neither of us seems to know what to say. He's not going to leave quietly. My stupid hormones just had to weaken and let him in a little.

"You want a beer or coffee?"

"Neither."

"Why are you really here?"

"Just wanted to see you were okay." He breaks eye contact first and looks away.

I shake my head. He really is an idiot sometimes. "You know we're okay. You and Hendrix followed us to my apartment, then here. And Bankz has ridden by twice in twenty minutes."

His head snaps back to me. "How do you know Bankz has been by?"

I laugh. His jealousy is kind of cute. It's annoying, too. "His Mustang has a distinctive sound."

"Okay." He nods, more to himself than me. "I've checked the backyard and the neighborhood. The Millers around the corner had a party. They're still rowdy."

The Millers do not like the Vikings. They're not church goers, either. Still, if a side has to be taken, they'll side with anyone against the club. They're known for causing problems of their own around town.

"If we have any problems, we'll let you know." My apartment would have been the quieter option.

The awkward silence falls between us again. Emily loudly fumbles around in the bathroom and turns the shower on. She and I are going to have to talk about her subtle skills, or lack thereof. Stealthy is not her thing.

"We need to talk."

Yeah. I knew that was coming. Kindness always leads to conversations.

"We shouldn't."

He takes a step closer. "Come on, Sparky. We can't keep going like this."

We can, but he's determined. Honestly, I'm a little tired of it and highly emotional tonight. "Okay. Tomorrow afternoon."

He looks away again and rubs the back of his neck. "Can't. We have Church tomorrow afternoon."

"Right." I nod and smack my lips. He doesn't know I overheard the guys talking about it at the clubhouse. "Club's always first."

His eyes lock with mine. "For most things, it is."

Ole' ladies, children, and family members get special privileges. The entire club will fight to protect them and show up when they need help. I'm not an ole' lady or any club member's family. His eyes hold a look of determination. The moment they soften, my heart does, too.

"Okay." I look away and nod. "We'll figure out something next weekend. The McLeods need us right now."

His shoulders drop as he releases a long breath. "You're right. They do. Next weekend." His eyes move back to mine. "But I'll call, text, and check on you in the meantime."

"That's fine." It's not like he's not already doing those things.

We look toward the bathroom door when the shower turns off. Emily moves around loudly again.

"I'll check the neighborhood one more time."

"Thank you."

He's a liar. He won't leave this neighborhood. His eyes will be on Emily's apartment all night.

Coty

"I appreciate that." And I do. Knowing he's watching over us makes me feel safe. I haven't felt safe in a long time.

"Night, Sparky." He lifts his hand to touch my face, but drops it to his side.

"Night, Coty."

I close the door and lock it. I turn to find Emily standing in the living room in the same clothes she had on earlier.

"You really should give him a chance." She doesn't wait for a reply and starts the coffee.

I should give Coty a chance. My problems aren't really his fault. Sadly, I'm too scared to try.

12
Coty

The clubhouse isn't as quiet as it was last night. We're not back to normal yet, though. The gloomy feeling isn't as heavy today. Our patched members are here, and a few of their ole' ladies. The ones with children stayed home. A couple of bunnies are here with the prospects at the pool tables.

Pops is at the bar as usual. He looks lost without Granddad. Dobbs is the only bartender here today. He's trying to keep Pops entertained. It would be nice to see Kayla behind the bar. She's better off staying with Emily today. Thankfully, they're still together since the bakery is closed on Sundays.

Worley finishes his beer and slaps Pops on the back. Dobbs will watch over his dad while we have our meeting. Our patched members follow Worley into Church. He closes the doors behind the last Viking before joining Mack and the rest of the officers down front. Mack sits in the center. Our President looks exhausted. I slide into the front row with Jack and Jay. They're the only three members of the McLeod family we've seen today.

"Vikings!" Mack calls out and taps the gavel. "Time for Church." The room immediately goes quiet. "We have a few things to discuss."

Worley takes over. "Last night was horrible. Nick and his computer friends have worked around the clock to take down as much as they can."

Nick sits at the edge of the officer's table with his laptop open. He glances up while still typing. "We expect the worst of the social media attack against us to last two or three weeks. The wonderful citizens of Willow Creek who hate us resubmit the videos and pictures within an hour of us taking them down. Hopefully, most will give up or get bored soon."

It's like every man in the room sighs. This town is insane. Half of them look for a reason to come after us. They do it from a distance with gossip and social media posts. None of them are brave enough to attack us head-on. Their hatred for the club makes no sense. In the forty years the Viking Warriors have been in Willow Creek, we've never attacked anyone. We don't sell drugs or guns. We own businesses and help out when someone is in need. These people have watched too many TV shows and movies. Most of those don't paint motorcycle clubs in a good light. Around here, if you have a bike and a cut, you're the bad guy.

Mack leans forward with his forearms on the table. "I reached out to Pastor Rhodes today. His secretary said the Pastor will make a formal statement soon. His family refuses to speak to a McLeod or club member."

Personally, I don't think Mack should've been the first to reach out. The formal statement concerns me. This won't be good if the Pastor isn't willing to talk with Mack. Sounds like they're going to play into the sympathy their family's getting on social media. It's just another thing to divide this town.

"We're going to get some backlash from this. So, until it dies down, don't go anywhere alone. That includes your ole' ladies and families," Worley says.

"We hope this doesn't get out of hand, but just in case, we'll assign rounds to everyone so we can watch over our club friends and the ones who live alone, " Big Papa, our Treasurer, adds.

As much as we don't want to believe this will get out of hand, it more than likely will. Watching over our families and friends is what we do every time there's trouble. My security assignment will be wherever Kayla is. When Jack and Lily return to the guest house, maybe she'll stay with them for a few days. I don't like her living alone.

Nick's phone dings. He quickly reads the message and locks eyes with Mack. "I hate to add to our problems, but three Midnight Mavericks just walked into Angie's." He clicks around on the laptop. "She put them at the first table in the back dining room. I have eyes on them now."

Nick has access to the security cameras at Angie's restaurant. She's had trouble break out in the restaurant because she's a friend of ours. Nick has a camera set up to watch the area where Angie seated the Mavericks. She puts possible troublemakers there and messages Nick.

"Do we need to send a couple of guys up there?" Jack asks.

"No," Mack replies quickly. "We have club business to tend to today. Nick's monitoring it for now. We'll only go if we have to."

As President, Mack's decisions are final. This one feels wrong. We always help when Angie calls. What happened at the church last night is important, but there's nothing we can do unless someone does something to us. Right now, it's just a lot of bad press and social media posts.

Having Midnight Maverick in Willow Creek is bad. I highly doubt it's a coincidence. They've bound to have seen the news and checked the social apps. Vikings and Mavericks have been club rivals from the beginning. I've never heard a good explanation for what started it. We can't prove it, but we believe the Mavericks are behind Jack's house being attacked and Lily getting shot. Knowing three Mavericks are in town makes me antsy.

"What do we need to tend to that's more important than helping Angie?" Leave it to Jay to ask. Angie has a bit of a soft spot for Jay. I don't know why, but she's always looked out for him.

"I'm glad you asked, son." Jay is really Mack's nephew. He's called Jay son since he was a kid. "Come up here." Mack walks around the table and motions for Jay to join him.

Jay, like the rest of us, has no idea what's going on. He looks to Jack for an answer. Jack shrugs. He's struggling to hold a straight face. The little twitch of the corner of his lips gives him away. Jack knows what's happening.

"Uncle Jacob?" Jay's not good with surprises or being put on the spot like this.

Mack puts an arm around Jay's shoulders and pulls him close. "Jason Alexander McLeod, I have loved you like a son since the moment you were born. You've grown into a fine man. You're loyal and give your all to this club."

Jay nods but doesn't speak. He's not good with being praised either. Jack's grin is about to split his face. I nudge him with my elbow. Whatever this is, why didn't he tell me?

"Just watch," Jack whispers.

Well, okay. What other choice do I have? I love Jack like a brother. Sometimes, I want to pop him upside the head.

Mack holds his right arm out at an angle that's a little behind him. He motions for one of the officers to come down front. "Sandman, you wanna join us?"

Several Vikings gasp. I'm one of them. No way. I lock eyes with Jack. He nods, and we silently laugh. Well, I'll be darn.

"Uncle Jacob, what's going on?" The way Jay's eyes bounce between his uncle and Sandman, he has a pretty good idea of what's happening.

"Vikings!" Mack smiles at Jay and turns to face the club members. "Sandman has been our Sergeant at Arms for over ten years. After what happened Thanksgiving night, he talked it over with his ole' lady and decided to step down. Sandman nominated Jay as his replacement."

"I second it," Worley says loudly.

From the excitement now flowing through the room, we're about to have a new Sergeant at Arms. At least something good will happen today.

"Vikings, we have a nomination and a second. Time to vote. All in favor of Jay McLeod being the Viking Warriors MC, Tennessee Chapter, Enforcer, say aye."

A unanimous round of ayes goes around the room.

"Anyone oppose?" Mack asks.

The room falls silent.

"Jay, the position is yours if you want it." Mack gives him a firm nod.

"Uncle Jacob, are you sure?" I'm…" Jay looks at Jack. "But…"

Jack joins his dad and cousin. "But I'm not President yet. Yeah. I know." Jack shakes his head. "I'm not ready for that step yet. You're ready for this, Jay. You were born ready for this." Jack shrugs one shoulder. "It doesn't matter that you make it to the table before I do. Take it, Jay. I want you to."

Sandman clamps a hand on Jay's shoulder. "I won't step down if you don't." He grins. "My ole' lady will be highly pissed at both of us if I don't." That's a scary thought. Jay should take it or watch his back. Sandman's ole' lady will be out for him. She loves pranks.

Jay looks from his family to the rest of his club brothers. We all nod, encouraging him to take the position. He and Jack always thought they'd become officers together. I admire Jack a little more for admitting he's not ready to be president. His father's shoes are big ones to fill. Not to worry. Mack's training Jack to take his place when the time's right.

Sandman holds his hand out. Jay takes it and smiles. "Thanks, Sandman. I hope I do half as good as you."

"Son, you'll be better." Sandman hands the officer's patch to Jay.

Jay reads it and snaps his head toward Mack. "Uncle Jacob?"

Mack smiles and looks at the club members again. "Vikings, welcome Blade, Jay McLeod, as your new club Enforcer."

The room erupts in whistles, cheers, and applause. This is an epic day for the Viking Warriors MC.

"Enforcer? Not Sergeant at Arms?" Jay asks when the cheering quietens down.

Mack puts an arm around Jay's shoulders again. "Son, with the way you love knives and how fiercely you protect our family and club, Enforcer fits you better."

He's not wrong. Jay is a whole other level of protection. He'll do the position justice.

"Vikings, get with me after the meeting. We'll set up times and areas for you to patrol," Worley hands Mack the gavel across the table.

"Bankz, Hendrix, head to Angie's and make sure she doesn't need help with the Mavericks." He points at them. "Don't start anything, though." They nod and leave. "Everyone else, keep your eyes peeled and report anything that feels off. Church's adjourned." Mack taps the gavel.

Everyone quickly surrounds Jay and ushers him to the bar for a drink. Jack walks out with me.

"I would have told you if there was time. Sandman talked to Dad about stepping down just before Church."

I'm not a teenage girl with hurt feelings. It's good to know, though. "It's fine, man. And you'll get to the table one day."

"We both will." He nods toward the bar. "You want a drink, or are you patrolling Edgewood Drive?"

I laugh. He knows me well. "Would you be mad?"

"Not at all, Rodeo. Go make sure your girl's safe."

Of course, Jack would understand. He almost lost Lily. Jack makes a path to the bar so I can congratulate Jay before I head out. I'll spend another night in my truck on Edgewood Drive.

13
Kayla

My week has been surprisingly calm. After agreeing to talk with Coty this weekend, he hasn't pushed for more. He hasn't disappeared, though. He texts several times a day and only calls once. He also shows up at nearly every place I go in town. He keeps his distance, giving me space. Guess I have a stalker. At least Coty isn't creepy. I know he's there, and it doesn't really bother me. When something's going on with the club, Mack assigns protection for their friends just in case. Naturally, Coty would volunteer to be my protection.

I stayed three nights at Emily's. By Tuesday afternoon, there were no major incidents around town, so I went home. I love Emily, and hanging out with her is great. After a year of living alone, I prefer being in my own place.

The Roadhouse didn't have any problems last night. The atmosphere was off, though. It was weird. I can't explain it. The customers were mostly from out of town. I'm not sure if the locals stayed away because they're mad at the McLeods or if people saw the news and showed up to see if something would happen. Only crazy people would put themselves in the middle of a feud. Is this a feud? Well, if something more happens, the McLeods won't start it.

Let's hope tonight goes smoothly, too. I'm looking forward to having the next three days off. My phone rings while I'm getting dressed for my closing shift at the Roadhouse. Surprisingly, it's a friend from college and not Coty.

"Hey, Kira."

"Kayla!" She screams so loud that I hold the phone away and switch it to speaker.

"Hey," I say again. "Long time, no talk."

Kira and I were roommates in college. We meet in Nashville a few times a year. We text more than we call. She only calls when she has something exciting going on.

"I know. We need a Nashville trip soon."

"Sounds good. How many bars you wanna hit?" I tease.

"We could paint Nashville red, or I have a better idea." I can practically see her wiggling with excitement.

"Oh." I'm almost afraid to ask. Her better ideas aren't better.

"Or you could come spend next weekend with me in Knoxville." Her voice is filled with excitement.

A weekend in Knoxville is not a better plan. Knoxville is where troubles happen. I'm not fond of going back there. I only drive through it when I have no choice.

"I have an even better idea. You can come stay with me for a few days. I could introduce you to a few sexy bikers." She teased me often for being part of a motorcycle club.

"I think not!" a male voice says sternly.

Who is that? His voice is familiar, but I can't place it. I know him. I can almost picture his face.

"Well, I'm going to have to pass." Kira giggles.

Oh, that's not good. She's only giddy when she's making bad decisions. The dude in the background is no doubt part of her newest bad decision.

"What's up, Kira?" She'll drag this out even more if I don't bluntly ask.

"I'm getting married!"

I groan and drop my head. Yep. It's another bad decision. The girl doesn't have an active cell left in her brain. Married? Kira Mitchell, her family's and half of Middle Tennessee's wild child, is getting married.

"Congratulations." I don't share in her excitement.

"You're my Maid of Honor, so I need you here next weekend to plan everything," she informs me.

Now, I know this is a horrible idea. "Kira, I have to work and check on my family. I can't just up and leave town on the weekends. I can't miss work to help you plan a wedding."

She knows I work in a bar. It's why we have always met in Nashville on a weeknight. I've already worked out my schedule with Bankz for the next two months. I need the extra tips for a down payment on a car. The part about checking on my family isn't true. We rarely talk.

"You're my Maid of Honor. I'm getting married two weeks from today. I need you here," Kira snaps.

Whoa. This is beyond a bad idea. For starters, she didn't ask me to be her Maid of Honor. She's mental and should be committed somewhere. Who plans a wedding in two weeks? And nothing good ever happens to me in Knoxville.

"Come on, Kayla. Please," she whines. "I don't have anybody else."

She would if she hadn't cut her entire family off. Of course, I can't say much. I have my family. We just don't get along. I pause and tap my fingers on the bathroom sink. Maybe I don't have my family.

"Kayla," she whines again.

Oh, good grief. I don't want to do it, but I don't want to lose a friend, either.

"Look. I can come during the week to help you plan. I'll talk to my boss and see if I can switch out days and get off for the wedding next Saturday. That's the best I can do on such short notice." Yes, I threw the last part in to make her feel guilty. It's not like she's not playing on my feelings.

"Yay! Thank you. Can you come this Tuesday?" She believes she's won. Maybe she has.

"Sure. I'll be there around noon, but I have to leave by six." She knows my usual days off. If I don't give her a timeframe, she'll have me there all night. An all-night stay in Knoxville is a really bad idea.

Coty

It's not like this is going to be a big fancy wedding. You can't plan a nice wedding in two weeks. It sounds more like a shotgun wedding to me. I stare at myself in the mirror. My mouth falls open, and my eyes widen. Oh no. Could Kira be pregnant? It would explain the rush. Oh, this is bad, so so bad.

"Thanks, Kayla. See you Tuesday." Kira ends the call.

Wow. I don't want to assume anything, but if Kira's pregnant, that's going to be a disaster. She could barely take care of herself in college. Her aunt paid her tuition balance after state and federal scholarships so she'd have a better life. Sadly, Kira wanted to party more than work for a degree and a promising career. I can't say anything there either. Oh well, I'll get all the details on Tuesday. It's Saturday night, the best night for tips. Work is calling my name. Well, tips are. I need that down payment.

I finish getting dressed and grab my keys. My phone rings again before I pull out of the driveway. It would have been better if this call were from Coty. My father's name lights up on the screen. Uh. I should throw it out the window.

"Hey, Dad."

"Kayla, you ok?" His tone is sharp, as always.

"I'm good. Just heading to work."

"Right." Of course, he's disappointed with me. "Saw the trouble on the news."

I roll my eyes and shake my head to no one. The trouble happened a week ago, and this is the first I've heard from anyone in my family.

"I'm good."

"Well." He huffs. "Your mom's planning a family dinner tomorrow. Be here by six." He abruptly ends the call.

Great. Just one more thing I don't want to do. I don't want to go to Knoxville. I don't want to be Kira's Maid of Honor. I seriously don't want to have dinner with my family. I don't want to talk to Coty Michaels. Thinking his name pauses my emotional spiral.

"Coty," I whisper.

Then again, maybe I wouldn't mind seeing him.

14
Coty

It's been a long week. Wish I could say it was boring and uneventful, but I can't. The news channels have stopped sharing the footage from the church's candlelight vigil. If Nick knows why they stopped, he's not saying.

The social media posts continue. Mack extended the order of not going out alone until things die down some more around town. It's a good thing, too. Willow Creek is a divided town. No fights have broken out. There have been several occasions where rude comments were shouted at our family members. Once again, no one says anything to a patched member. Our family members don't respond. They walk away. They're getting tired of it, though. It's only a matter of time before someone explodes.

Kayla arrived at work a couple of hours ago. One of the prospects followed her to the Roadhouse while I helped out at the Den. Jack's family is trying to get back to some sense of normal. Granddad is at the bar with Pops tonight. Jack and his dad are watching over the clubhouse. Nick was a little concerned with the crowd at Angie's tonight. It's where I'm heading. Bankz and Hendrix have things under control at the

Roadhouse. They have eyes on Kayla at all times. I'll head there once I'm sure Angie doesn't need help.

Angie has a pretty big crowd tonight. I pull into the lot and park a few spaces from the front door. The side lot looks full. There must be a party going on inside.

"Rodeo!" Angie hurries from behind the counter to hug me when I step inside. "Good to see you."

"Good to see you, too." She sees me about twice a week. Her enthusiasm being this high might mean there's a problem.

"How about a bacon cheeseburger tonight?" She grabs a set of silverware and a menu.

Okay. I was gone for two years and have only been back a few months. I'm a little rusty on hidden codes, if this is one. Bacon cheeseburgers are Jay's favorite meal.

"How about your famous fried chicken with mashed potatoes and fried okra?" I tease.

"Good choice." Angie pauses at the lower end of the front counter and hands the unnecessary menu and my order to one of her servers. Her eyes dart over her shoulder. "You know 'em? Are they Mavericks?"

I glance at the front table in the back dining room. Two heavy-set men with scruffy beards are sharing a pizza and a couple of beers. Who comes to a country-style restaurant and orders pizza? Idiots, of course.

"Have they caused any trouble?"

"Nothing I can prove. They stare at a few tables, making customers uncomfortable. Two families asked to change their orders to go and left. They called and told me about it once they were in their cars."

That's not good. It's not anything we can do anything about. I send a quick text to Nick. Hopefully, he can ID them.

"I don't know their names. Unless something changed while I was gone, they're not Mavericks. I've seen them at the races at The Field, but that was years ago."

The party in the back starts singing Happy Birthday. I look over Angie's head. Great. The Rhodes family is celebrating their oldest daughter, Daphene's, birthday. The two men watch the party with interest. Their interest sends a chill down my spine.

"That's another problem." Angie hands me a glass of sweet tea. "Those two make Matthew Rhodes nervous."

I take a sip of tea and casually search the party for Matthew. It looks like half the church members are with them tonight. Sure enough, Matthew is extremely uncomfortable.

"Well, Angie. I'm sure you know the Rhodes family really hates us right now. Whatever their beef is with Matthew isn't our problem." The preacher's son is a jerk. I have no problem letting him get what's coming to him. She should have called the cops, not us.

"I'm well aware, Rodeo." She says, like I'm an idiot. "But this sure is."

I follow her to the back dining room. She escorts me to a two-top table near the employee door to the kitchen. Customers rarely sit here. Vikings do when we're here monitoring a situation for her, like tonight. One of those seats is already taken.

Angie pauses a few feet away, out of hearing range. "He showed up about half an hour ago." She turns and places her hand on my arm. "He hates Matthew Rhodes. Please, don't let him do anything stupid."

"Don't worry. I got him," I assure her.

"Both of your plates will be out shortly." She relaxes a little and goes into the kitchen.

I consider calling Jack. His family's still struggling and needs him. This wild-card McLeod might need him, too. Hopefully, I can handle this. If I can't, I'll call Hendrix. He's closer.

I pull the chair out and sit down. "How's it going, Jay?"

"I hate him." Jay absent-mindedly stirs the straw around in his glass of tea. His eyes never leave the preacher's son.

We seriously need to figure out what happened between these two. There was friction between them before Jack and I left. This is pure hate. Jay doesn't go this dark on anyone without a good reason. From the sound of the knife flicking open and closed under the table, this isn't the normal Jay McLeod. He's Blade, a dark force I don't recommend people meet. One wrong move, and Matthew Rhodes may die tonight.

Yeah. It's a good thing Angie called Nick. Jack needs to know. I pull up his name and start typing.

Jay lays his hand over the phone screen. "Don't call him. I'm fine."

He's not fine. Still, I stop typing and hold my phone below the table while Angie brings out our plates. She sees who I was trying to message and winks. Well, maybe I haven't forgotten how to talk in code and hidden gestures.

"Can I get you boys anything else?"

"No, ma'am. We're good." I nudge Jay with my foot.

"No ma'am. This is great." Jay gives her a tight smile. He would never intentionally be rude to Angie.

Finley notices us and leaves her date. Well, maybe she needs Angie. As long as Jay's been here, I'm sure she's seen him. Before she reaches us, Matthew grabs her arm.

"Don't mess this up, Finley," Matthew says.

"Just what am I messing up, Matthew?" Finley glares at her brother.

Jay slides to the edge of his chair, ready to pounce. He's been waiting for a reason to go after Matthew. Being rude to your sister, or any woman, will have a Viking all over a man. Being the preacher's son won't save Matthew from Jay.

"You were told to stay away from them. Now, get back to your boyfriend before this one runs off, too." Matthew slightly pushes Finley toward their table.

Jay's on his feet. Angie and I move in front of him. If we weren't in a public place, I'd let Jay loose on this jerk.

Finley pulls her arm away and steps back. "You get back to your girlfriend," she snaps. Whoa. Good for her.

"Easy, Blade. Not here," I whisper.

"I can drag him outside." Jay doesn't whisper.

Matthew glances at the two men across the room. He slightly puffs out his chest. Sadly for him, it doesn't make him look threatening. "Look, McLeod. You and your family need to stay away from me and mine."

"Can't. Won't." Jay growls deep.

Matthew swallows hard. Fear briefly flashes in his eyes.

Angie sighs. She turns and smiles at Finley. "Finley, sweetie. Can I get you anything?"

"Yes, Miss Angie. We'd like more biscuits and honey butter, please." She cuts her eyes at her brother. "Mom asked for them."

Matthew huffs and storms back to their table. It's the smartest move he's made tonight. I release Jay when his body relaxes. Whew. That had me worried. There's no way I could've stopped him if he went after Matthew. Jay's taller, bigger, and definitely stronger than I am.

"Would your family like more jams and jellies too?" Angie's always the server, no matter how much she wants to tell people off. Not Finley, though. She's the sweetest member of her family.

"Yes, ma'am. A mixture, if you don't mind. I'd really love extra blackberry, please." Finley's eyes lock with Jay's before moving to mine. "Thank you, Coty. I hope you have a lovely evening." She goes back to her family and pretends to enjoy their celebration.

Jay and I return to our table. The food looks great, but neither of us has an appetite. I flag one of the servers down and ask for two to-go boxes.

"You wanna go to the Roadhouse with me?" It's best to get Jay out of here.

He shakes his head. "I'm going to make sure everyone gets home safely. I don't trust Matt, and I sure don't trust those two." He glares at the two men.

"Racers?"

Jay shrugs one shoulder. "Sometimes. They bet more than they race."

Awe. Matthew must owe them money. The preacher's son used to slip off to The Field during the summer months. We definitely need to stay out of this. I couldn't care less if Matthew's debtors are hunting him down. I have better things to do tonight. My phone dings with a text.

Sparky: *I have to have dinner with my parents tomorrow. Rain Check.*

I toss my phone on the table and slouch down in my chair. If I go to the Roadhouse now, I'll cross lines and demand she talk to me. I vowed to do this at her pace. I'm an idiot. I'm trying to be gentle, like Jack is with Lily. I now understand his struggle. Being patient will drive a man insane.

"Looks like I'm with you tonight." If I can't have what I want, I can at least make sure my friend doesn't end up in jail.

15
Kayla

Sundays are supposed to be for relaxing. I usually sleep in since I close Saturday nights at the Roadhouse. Well, technically, it's Sunday morning. The bar closes at 2 am on the weekends. My afternoons are spent on the couch with a tray of snacks while watching a movie, or at the Viking Den. Since Coty's been back, I've watched lots of movies.

I arrive at my parents' house at six on the dot. Arriving early to spend quality time with my parents is a big no. It's doubtful they know the definition of quality time anyway. Of course, my brother was already here. He's probably been here all afternoon.

David is the golden child of our family. Nearly everyone in town loves my brother. Our parents sometimes message me updates about him. It's okay if they don't. David's wonderful accomplishments make it through the gossip circles in this town on a regular basis. I try to tune it out. It makes me sick listening to how great my brother is. It wouldn't be so bad if they didn't give me the little side glance as if to ask, *What happened to you?* Yes, I'm the family screw up.

"Hey, little sister." David meets me at the door before I can knock.

"Hey." I hang my coat on the hanger by the door. "How was your week?"

"It was good. Yours?"

"It was okay." Making small talk is the worst.

Laughter comes from the kitchen. My parents have guests. Oh wow. I wasn't expecting company. I stop and look up at David. Laughter isn't common in this house.

"Aunt Ellen is staying a few days," David answers my unspoken question.

Great. Dad's sister is here. Her charming personality is as awesome as Dad's. I should leave now.

"Come on." My brother sees my fight-or-flight kick in and ushers me to the kitchen.

"Kayla, there you are." Aunt Ellen rushes over and hugs me.

Whoa. Who is this alien, and what has she done with my aunt? She's never hugged me before. Well, not that I can remember.

"Nice of you to join us, dear." Mom shoves silverware into my hands. She shows no emotion whatsoever.

Okay. Guess I'm helping. "Yeah. Thanks for inviting me."

After placing a set of silverware by each plate, I take my usual seat on Mom's right. I'm on this side of the table by myself. David is across from me with Aunt Ellen to his right, next to Dad. The table is covered with dishes like this is Thanksgiving or Christmas.

The meal is awkward. I don't know why they invited me. Dad and his sister talk about her life in New York. Mom and David talk about his new job at a local winery. I didn't realize being a winemaker was such a big deal. No one speaks to me. It's fine. The faster I clean this plate, the faster I can get out of here. This family fiasco is almost over.

"Well, Kayla. What's up with you?" Aunt Ellen asks.

"What?" I cover my mouth with my hand, almost choking on my food.

"I asked, What are you up to these days?" Unlike my other family members, Aunt Ellen looks me in the eye and waits for a reply.

"Oh." I dab my napkin to my lips. "My friend, Kira, is getting married in two weeks."

"Oh, how lovely." Aunt Ellen isn't impressed.

"I'm her Maid of Honor," I add. It was a stupid move.

"You mean Kira Mitchell? Your college roommate?" Mom asks.

"Yes. Her." I take a sip of water, wishing I'd kept my mouth shut.

"Interesting," Dad sneers.

"Is something wrong with this Kira?" Aunt Ellen looks around the table at each of us.

"Let's just say everything and forget her," Dad replies.

"She got Kayla in so much trouble." Mom rolls her eyes.

"Oh." Aunt Ellen sits up straighter. "I guess it's a good thing I showed up then."

I glance up at my brother. He stares back as he takes a bite of ham. I snap my head toward Mom, then to Dad. Finally, I settle on Aunt Ellen.

"What are you talking about?" All four of them are in on whatever this is. I'm sure of it.

"Well." Aunt Ellen lays her napkin on the table and shifts her body to face me. "I'm here to hire you for my company."

"You live in New York," I remind her.

She nods. "I do, and I was just promoted to department manager. I need an office manager."

"New York out of office managers?" I ask, snarkily.

"Kayla, mind your manners," Mom scolds.

"I'm here to offer the job to a family member. If I remember correctly, it was your dream to work in an office in New York." Aunt Ellen tilts her head. "It would be nice to see that degree of yours and the money my brother paid for it, to go to good use."

Ah, yes. There's my snooty aunt. Guess the aliens didn't want to keep her after all. With her attitude, I can't say I blame them. But did they have to bring her back here? Pluto would be a lovely planet for Aunt Ellen.

"I don't have a degree," I inform her.

"What?" Her hand flies to her chest. She turns to Dad, absolutely horrified. "You let her drop out."

"He stopped paying for my tuition during my third year." I managed to finish the spring semester. I wasn't able to make enough that summer to go back for my final year. Three years and no MBA in the end.

"Randall, why would you do that?" She glares at her brother.

"I stopped when the rest of us got months of videos and pictures of her partying all over Knoxville with this Kira and a couple of guys. Every night of every weekend. Drinking, drugs, and men are not what I was paying for." Dad's voice rises with every sentence.

"I never did drugs, and it was one guy," I mumble. He doesn't hear me, or doesn't care.

Dad points at me. "I told you that Christmas, to clean your act up if you wanted me to pay for college." He shakes his head. "You didn't listen. For three weeks, pictures and videos came constantly. You were either at bars in Knoxville or here, partying with those bikers. You made your choice. I made mine and pulled your funding."

Wow. Way to stab me again, Dad. Yes, I partied. Yes, I was drinking. No, I never did drugs. Those around me did them. Yes, there was a man, only one. A mean one I wished I'd never met. I kept coming back to the Den, hoping Coty was home.

"I can't hire her without a degree. My company insists on them," Aunt Ellen says.

"Can't she just go back and finish the last year?" David asks.

"I'm not paying for it. Knoxville is the last place she needs to go." Dad throws his napkin on the table.

"There are more colleges than Knoxville," David points out. Is my brother actually trying to help me?

"That's true," Mom agrees quickly. She sounds hopeful for the first time in years.

Aunt Ellen taps her finger to her chin. "I could take her back with me and get her into a college in New York. She could come work for me after graduation." Ah, so that's their plan.

I slowly push away from the table and stand. "Y'all see me, right? I'm right here. I'm twenty-five. Y'all can't dictate my life."

I didn't go to college right out of high school like my brother and most teens do. I was twenty when I signed up. Two years ago, Dad's decision ended my dream of becoming an office manager.

"We just want what's best for you," Mom pleads.

"I'm not going to New York. I wasn't doing everything you think I was doing. If you wanted better for me, you shouldn't have pulled my school funding. My grades were good, but I don't want that life anymore."

Ignoring their protests and cheap shots at how badly I'm making another mistake, I grab my coat and walk out the door. I'll never be good enough for them. It's fine. I don't care and highly doubt they do. They have David. They don't need me.

16
Coty

As much as I want to, I don't drive down Mauldin Drive. Kayla's father hates everything about the Viking Warriors MC and everybody connected to us. Randall Chambers' disgust for bikers isn't spared from his own daughter either, because she's our friend. Well, let's face it. I think of Kayla as more than a friend. Too bad I didn't realize it until after I left. Maybe I did realize it. I just didn't want to accept it as more than a crush at the time.

I'm not welcome near her parents' house. Her father told me so years ago. It's another reason I never pushed to see if my feelings for Kayla were more than friendship. Families play a big part in relationships around here. Some parents encourage their children, while others destroy any chance their children have. Kayla's parents are the latter. It's probably why her brother doesn't date anyone seriously either.

My club brothers had no problem helping me out today. Parker, Cole, and Hendrix drove by the Chambers' residence every fifteen to twenty minutes. On Parker's second pass, about the hour mark, Kayla pulled out of her parents' driveway ahead of him. Her erratic driving concerned him enough to call me immediately. Something happened at dinner, just as I knew it would. She's either mad or upset. Both make me want to drive to her parents' house and punch someone.

When she turned onto the street to her apartment, Parker and the others went to the clubhouse, and I took over. I was halfway there, anyway. I'm leaning more toward her being upset. I've patrolled her street for nearly an hour. She hasn't called or texted me. I've been sitting outside her apartment for another twenty minutes. I don't think she knows I'm here. If she were mad, she'd have already stormed out here and told me off by now if she did.

My phone dings. I reach for it on the passenger seat without taking my eyes off her front door. There have been many nights I've watched apartment A17. I glance down at the message.

Sparky: *Coty.*

Has she spotted me? The curtains haven't moved.

Me: *Hey, Sparky.*

Sparky: *Where*

Sparky: *Are you?*

Her front door doesn't open.

Me: *Why?*

Me: *You miss me?*

Yeah, that one was a little risky.

I watch between my phone screen and the front door. No bubble with the three little dots pops up. The front door doesn't open. Something's wrong. I feel it. Once again, I'm an idiot. I should have already checked on her. I jump out of the truck and run to the door.

"Kayla!" I knock loudly.

I know she's inside.

"Kayla!" I yell and pound harder on the door.

The door jerks open, and she stumbles into me. My arms automatically wrap around her to keep her from falling face-first on the concrete slab.

"Coty!" She looks up and exclaims a little too happily. "You're here."

"Yeah, darlin. I am."

"I knew you were close." Her words are slurred, and she slowly pats my cheek several times. "Always are."

Oh, good gracious. She's drunk. Great. Yep, I'm an idiot. I could have prevented this if I'd knocked on her door an hour ago. A couple of her neighbors peek out their windows. No one needs to see her like this.

"Come on, Sparky. Let's get you inside."

"Oh, yeah. Side. We can watch movies."

"A movie sounds good."

She won't make it through a movie, but thankfully, I get her inside without a huge scene. Hopefully, her neighbors won't share what little they witnessed around town. Gossip can destroy someone's life fast in Willow Creek.

"You want beer?" She stumbles toward the kitchen.

I scoop her up and carry her to the couch. "I think you've had enough."

"No." She pushes against my chest. "Stop telling me what I need, what I want. I decide."

Okay. Reading between the lines here, I'm guessing her parents told her what she should be doing with her life. No big surprise there. They more than likely pointed out her faults, too. I'm not the only idiot tonight.

"Okay, Sparky. I'll get you a beer. Wait here."

She lifts her arm and points at the ceiling. "That's more like it."

I grab the last two beers from the fridge. There's no carton, so I don't know how many she's already had. My guess is a lot. A whiskey bottle and a shot glass sit on the counter. Great. She's probably mixed drinks and will be sick by morning. If I could pour half of one of these out and fool her, I would. My best bet is to settle her down. When she relaxes, she'll pass out.

"Coty! Oh, Coty!"

I sigh and go back to the living room. She's not ready to pass out, yet.

"Here you go, Sparky."

She takes the beer and pats the couch. "Sit. Don't be rude."

Well, I can't be rude now, can I? I'm not about to pass up a chance to be close to her. I feel like a jerk doing this while she's drunk.

"What are we watching?" I sit next to her and look around for the remote.

"Nothing, silly." She falls back and giggles. "The TV's not on."

No, it's not. She's clearly forgotten that she mentioned watching a movie. This is going to be a long night.

"Okay. We can just talk." Well, no, we shouldn't. She's not in any state of mind to carry on a conversation.

"No talk. Talk hurts," she pouts and wiggles against my side.

I catch the bottle of beer and set it on the coffee table with mine before she drops it. She's closer to passing out than I thought.

"We can just sit."

"No sit. Couch hurts. I wanna go to bed." She struggles to get up.

I lift us off the couch and guide her to her room. It's a one-bedroom apartment, making finding her room easy. I've had a few friends who lived in this apartment complex over the years. The floor plans are nothing fancy.

She walks to the side of the bed and pulls her shirt over her head. For someone so drunk, she has no problem stripping out of her clothes. I groan and close my eyes. Why? Why did she have to do this while she's drunk? I want to appreciate every curve of her body, but not like this. Oh, the universe totally hates me.

"Help me," she cries.

I open my eyes to find her struggling to pull the covers back. She's beyond drunk. The covers should be the easy part.

"Hold on. I got it."

I quickly pull the sheet and comforter back. She slips under them without any more problems.

"Thank you." She blinks up at me. "Why you standing there?"

"What?"

She pats the spot next to her. "Sleep, Coty."

"But.." I can't do this. "I'll go to the couch."

"Please."

My head falls back. Yes, the universe hates me. I'm going to regret this in the morning. I slide my boots off and hang my cut on one of the bed posts. I lay down, fully clothed.

She grabs the hem of my t-shirt and lifts it up. "Off."

Okay. The shirt is all I'm taking off, though. I pull it over my head and drop it on the floor.

"Better," she whispers and snuggles against my side with her head on my chest.

Any other night, this would be Heaven. Tonight, it's pure torture. The word *wrong* repeats over and over in my head. Maybe now she'll be satisfied enough to relax and fall asleep. It's not my luck, though. I wrap my hand around hers to keep her fingers from moving across my chest.

"Go to sleep, Sparky," I whisper.

Her lips lightly press against my skin. Nope. She's not listening. I have to call on strength I didn't know I had. Staying still is so hard. I want to wrap my arms around her and pull her to me. More strength is needed as her lips trail light kisses up my chest, my neck, and to my cheek.

"Kayla, we shouldn't."

"That's exactly why we should."

My protests are lost when she presses her lips to mine. I'm a jerk, a big one. I don't force her to stop. I gently wrap my arms around her and let her have control of the kiss. My lips move with hers until she slows. With a light moan, she stops. Her head slips to my chest, and her breathing evens out. Finally, she's asleep. My struggle isn't over. Every part of my body is fully aware and awake. And I can't move.

17
Kayla

Oh. My. Gosh. My head's pounding before I open my eyes. Just how drunk did I get last night? I haven't been drunk in months. I groan and stretch my arms and legs. They meet resistance. Whoa. Something is holding me down. My eyes pop open, and I glance down. There's an arm around my waist, and a body is spooning mine.

No. No. No. This is not happening. What did I do last night? Who did I do it with? Oh, gosh. I may throw up right here on the side of the bed. This is not good. This is my apartment and my bed. I came straight home after leaving my parents' house. I can't just slip out while he's asleep. I would do that if I could.

Slowly, I glance over my shoulder. Coty? Oh, no. No. No. No. This did not happen. Coty Michaels cannot be in my bed. He can't have his body wrapped around mine.

"Coty!" I jump out of bed. Cold air hits my skin. I gasp and quickly cover my mouth with my hand. I'm naked. Completely naked. "Coty!" I scream again and jerk the comforter off the bed. I quickly wrap it around me.

"Huh?" His eyes pop open. "What's wrong?" He sits up and jerks his head from side to side, looking for the danger.

"You're in my bed!"

"Yeah." He rubs his hands over his face and yawns.

"You can't be in my bed." I point to his bare chest. "You don't have a shirt on." I sink into the comforter. "Please, tell me you're not naked, too."

He lifts the sheet and looks up with his lips pressed together. He is. Oh no.

"No. No. No." I pace near the foot of the bed. "Please tell me we didn't. Please."

"Sparky, calm down." He holds up one hand.

I whirl around to face him. "Calm down? Calm down?" Oh, I may stab this fool. "You did not just tell me to calm down. We did. Didn't we?"

"Uh, maybe?"

"Maybe? You don't know?"

"Look." He slides out of bed with the sheet around him. "Whatever happened, it can't be *that* bad."

My laughter turns to panicked breaths and tears. "Yes, it can. It is! We didn't do this." Oh, yes, we did. "How can you not remember? We couldn't have been *that* drunk. Oh my gosh. Why?"

"Settle down, and we'll figure this out." He steps around the foot of the bed.

"No!" I hold one hand out. "Don't come near me." I point to the door. "Get out."

"What? You can't be serious." His eyes narrow. Oh, yeah, buddy. We've got problems here.

I nod. "Oh, I'm dead serious. Get out!" I demand.

"You can't just throw me out." He has no right to be angry. "You don't remember anything. So, why's it all my fault?"

"I was drunk, Coty."

He rubs the back of his neck. "Yeah, you were. I'm sorry."

"Sorry? You're sorry? A little late now. Don't you think? Tell me you used protection."

"I..." He looks around like he's lost.

"No. No, you didn't." I suck in a deep breath. "Get out. Get out, now." I can't hold back the tears.

"Sparky, let's talk about this.

"Get out!" I scream.

"Kayla."

Nope. We're not talking. "Get your clothes and get out now, or I'll shoot you."

"You wouldn't. You don't mean that. You're just shocked and confused."

Oh, I'm more than shocked and confused. I'm pissed.

"Oh, I most definitely mean it. Get out now, Coty." I jerk the nightstand drawer and pull out my 22.

"Kayla?" At least now he sounds worried. Only took a gun to show him I'm serious.

I turn and aim the gun at him. "Leave. Now, or I'll shoot."

"Okay." He scrambles around on the floor for his jeans and quickly slides them on. "I'm going. We'll talk about this when you calm down."

"Oh, I'm calm now." I'm really not. "I want you out of my apartment."

"I'm going." He pulls his t-shirt over his head and snatches his cut from the bedpost. "Just don't shoot me."

I follow him to the living room with the gun still in my hand. I don't have it pointed directly at him anymore. As upset as I am, I might accidentally pull the trigger.

He opens the door with his boots in one hand and turns around. "Kayla, please."

"No." I don't let him finish. "This was wrong. We shouldn't have." I swipe the back of my hand under my nose. "Just go."

"We really should talk."

"No." I raise the gun. I would never shoot him. He doesn't know that, though. "Go, and don't stalk me anymore."

"Fine." He steps backward out the door. "When you're ready to talk, you know where to find me." He turns, leaves the door wide open, and walks to his truck barefoot.

After I hear him drive out of the parking lot, I close the door and lock the deadbolt. I press my forehead against the door and let the tears fall.

How did I have sex with him and not remember it? I've had a crush on him since I was thirteen. I'm my own worst enemy. Why did I freak out so badly?

Unable to stop crying, I go back to the bedroom and sit on the edge of the bed. My life is a mess. I'm the black sheep of my family. I'm a college dropout and will never get the job I always wanted. I'm emotionally broken. That's my fault. The man I want, I just spent the night with him and threatened to shoot him for it. Maybe Harley McLeod isn't the only one who needs therapy.

I put the gun back into the nightstand drawer. The safety was on. There was no way I would have shot Coty. He's an idiot for wanting to talk to me with a gun pointed at him. Eventually, he'll hate me, too, so it won't matter. But what do I do now? Sitting here wrapped in my comforter and crying won't solve anything.

The picture of Kira and me on my dresser mirror catches my eye. Kira. I can't get anything right in my life. However, I can be there to support my friend. I don't have to approve of her decision to support her. I jump from the bed and quickly shove some clothes into my travel bag. After a quick shower to wash away my latest mistake, I'll drive to Knoxville a day early.

I pause in the bathroom and stare at myself in the mirror. Last night shouldn't have happened. Still, it feels wrong to call it a mistake. For now, I need to put some actual distance between Coty and me. If I hurry, I'll be able to get out of Willow Creek without him knowing.

18
Coty

Well, that didn't go well. What was I expecting, though? For her to wake up happy and realize we belong together? Yeah, in the back of my mind, that's what I hoped would happen. Was I a jerk last night? Did I cross a line? Yep, both are true.

Kayla woke up more than once last night, a little handsy. She had way too much to drink. I should have gone to the couch after she'd fallen asleep the first time. The disaster now is my fault. I'll take full responsibility for whatever the fallout may be.

All the training I've had on how to handle an angel didn't help me last night. It all went right out the window. Soft, gentle, and kind disappeared. Well, not completely. I remember every moment. She doesn't remember any of it.

The first few times, I told her no and was able to coax her back to sleep. Then she got me in that half-awake, half-asleep state where I thought I was dreaming. I tried to coax her back to sleep when I realized it was real. She insisted she wasn't drunk anymore and repeatedly asked me to make love to her. Hormones and emotions won, and I made love to her. Only, she doesn't remember it. It's still my fault. I was the sober one.

The drive to the clubhouse was on autopilot. It's natural for this to be the first place my mind takes me. The gate doesn't open when I pull up. It's rare for me to have to speak to whoever is in the guardhouse.

Ross steps out and walks up to my window. He's watching the road behind me. "What'd you do?"

"Huh?" I glance up at the rearview mirror. Great. The Sheriff is sitting behind me. "Don't know." I didn't even know he was there.

It's possible I was driving recklessly or even speeding. I don't remember how I got here. I remember last night, though. A second Sheriff's car pulls in, and then a third. None of them has their blue lights on. I must have really messed up.

"Ah, man." I rub my hands up and down my face. What did I do?

"This ain't good, Rodeo." Ross glares at the cops.

Yeah, no kidding. I don't say that out loud. This ole' timer will reach in the truck and punch me out cold.

"If they arrest me, have one of the guys get my truck inside."

Ross nods once. He keeps his eyes on the cops. He has his phone out with an open call to Worley. By now, Nick is monitoring the situation. Sheriff Bowers gets out and walks up to my window.

"Morning, gentlemen." Nathan looks between Ross and me.

"Morning, Sheriff. What did I do?" I ask.

"You been drinking, Rodeo?" His eyes settle on me. "Awful early in the morning for that."

"No, Sheriff. I'm not drunk. If I'm being arrested, just tell me."

"I've been behind you for about two miles. You swerved a little, but never crossed the lines. I didn't see the need to pull you over for it."

"So, this is just a friendly little escort to make sure Rodeo got home safely?" Ross cannot stand cops.

Nathan's eyes flick to Ross. "It's not. I'm here to see the McLeods."

"Is this business?" Ross leans his head to the side to look past the Sheriff at the other two cars. "Or, a friendly visit?" Ross straightens up and locks eyes with the Sheriff. This fool is going to get arrested if he doesn't drop his attitude. "I'm guessing it's not the latter."

"You would be correct. I have a warrant, Ross." Nathan crosses his arms. "You can let us in, or I'll be back with a few more warrants. One to search the entire property and every vehicle on it."

"Let him in, Ross!" Worley yells through the phone.

"Fine," Ross grumbles as he walks back to the guardhouse and opens the gate.

"We'll follow you in, Rodeo." Nathan taps my open window twice. "Pay attention while driving from now on."

"Yeah, sure thing," I whisper and pull forward. I pull into a space in front of the clubhouse. I'm not about to lead them to the side entrance where the offices are.

Jack opens the front door before the three Sheriff cars are parked. He narrows his eyes at me while I put on my boots. I shake my head. I don't know why the cops are here. I sure don't have time to explain why I drove here with no shoes on. Not that my friend can see I'm what I'm doing.

Sheriff Bowers reaches the door as I do. "Jack, I need to see your family."

"Morning, Sheriff. Right this way." Jack leads the way to the bar and stands next to his dad.

Being Monday morning, there aren't a lot of members here. Nick sits at the bar with Granddad and Pops. His laptop is open in front of him, as always. Jay's behind the bar, pouring everyone a cup of coffee. After all, as the Sheriff pointed out, it's a little early to be drinking. You wouldn't think bikers could make good coffee. Jack and Jay could open a coffee shop if they wanted to. Biker Baristas. I snicker at the thought. Jack cuts his eyes at me. If anyone else noticed, they don't react.

Naturally, Worley's here. He rarely leaves Mack's side. Big Papa is here, too. His wife is in the kitchen. The prospects are lounging around on the couches by the pool tables. Nobody's playing. The club bunnies are at their house, about five miles from here. Jack's grandmother refuses to let them live on club property. Two prospects guard their house at all times.

"Sheriff." Mack doesn't extend his hand. "Heard you wanted to see us and have a warrant."

"I do," Nathan admits. Four deputies flank his sides and scan the room. "Where's the rest of your family, Mack?"

That's an odd question. All the men are here. A chill runs up my spine.

"Well, Maci is at college in Knoxville. Harley's been visiting friends since New Year's," Mack replies.

"Friends?" Nathan lifts an eyebrow.

The entire town is speculating about where Harley McLeod is. The rumors are outrageous. She hasn't run off with a biker to another club. A few get it right, but not the details. She's in rehab, but not in Tennessee. I'm sworn to secrecy about her location. Jack hasn't told Lily where his sister is yet. I'm not sure if Mack has told his wife.

"She's out of town. Is this about Harley?" Jack asks.

"No. And the rest of the family?" Nathan looks around the Den. Nobody's moved from their spots.

"Logan and Everly are at school. My wife and mother are in the kitchen, cooking breakfast. What's this about, Sheriff?" Mack's getting impatient.

"Do you mind asking the ladies to step out here, please?" Nathan asks.

The cold feeling runs up my spine again. Nothing about this little visit is normal.

"Why?" Jack demands. I move closer to his side.

Mack glares at Sheriff Bowers for a long moment. Finally, he dips his chin to Jay. Without a word, Jay slips through the door behind the bar to the kitchen. He escorts his grandmother and aunt to the Den. Lil Mama follows, drying a coffee mug with a dish towel.

"What's going on?" Nanny wraps her arms around Mack's waist and leans against him.

Sheriff Bowers pulls a long, folded piece of paper from the inside pocket of his coat. "I wanted you all here so we can get the arguments out of the way upfront, and I don't have each of you descending on the Sheriff's Office all day."

Okay. I see his point, but the Sheriff has underestimated the situation. It's obvious a member of the McLeod family is about to be arrested. The McLeods have family issues like most families do. Still, they're a close-knit family when it comes down to it. They fully support and defend each other. However, if the McLeod, I think, is getting arrested, there's not enough of us here to hold back the rest of the family. The Sheriff doesn't have enough deputies to stop them either.

"Oh, for crying out loud. What did we do?" Nana tosses her hand up. Granddad pulls his wife over to one of the bar stools.

Sheriff Bowers offers the warrant to Mack. "I don't want to do this." The four deputies move closer to the McLeod family. Nathan's eyes move to Jack's mother. "Evelyn McLeod, we have a warrant for your arrest."

And just as I expected, the room explodes.

Jack steps in front of his parents and jabs his finger at the Sheriff. "That's not happening."

"What did she do?" Jay demands.

"You're not taking my wife." Mack moves Nanny behind him.

The prospects move closer. The deputies pull their weapons. This is getting out of hand fast.

"Look!" Sheriff Bowers takes a step forward and raises his voice. "I have a warrant for her arrest. I have to take her. If I don't, the DA will call the FBI in. They'll bring SWAT teams here with warrants to search the entire two hundred acres, and they'll arrest the rest of you."

"You're not taking my wife," Mack yells again.

Nanny slips past her husband and son. "They have to. I hit the preacher's wife with that candle holder."

Two deputies grab Nanny's arms. The entire McLeod family moves.

"Don't," Sheriff Bowers orders.

"Stop them!" Nanny screams.

On her request, Worley grabs Mack and holds him back. I grab Jack. It takes all my strength to hold on to him. Three prospects grab Jay. They need help as much as I do.

"No!" Lil Mama runs forward and throws the cup she was drying. It shatters at the Sheriff's feet. "You're not taking my friend. Arrest that good-for-nothing preacher's wife! She asked for it! It should have been something harder than a metal candleholder. Weak pansy if that hurt her. Might need to wrap her up in bubble wrap."

"No, Dar. Don't." Nanny's plea comes too late.

"Take her, too," Sheriff Bowers orders the other two deputies.

They quickly handcuff Lil Mama.

Granddad has to hold Big Papa back. Nana goes to Jay and wraps her arms around his waist. One look into his grandmother's tear-filled eyes settles Jay down.

"Darlene Banks, you're under arrest, too." Sheriff Bowers turns to Mack. "We'll work this out at the station."

"You're a sorry excuse for a sheriff." Mack pulls Worley forward at least two feet, trying to get to his wife.

"Please, Mack," Nanny cries. "Don't fight them. Just get our lawyer and follow us."

Mack loses most of his fight. "Okay, love. We're right behind you."

Nanny looks over at Lil Mama. "You shouldn't have."

"I go where you go," Lil Mama says proudly. She glares up at the two deputies leading her out. "But I won't go quietly."

And she doesn't. She yells and tells the deputies just how awful they are, and I'm not repeating the things she says about the Rhodes family. Oh, I agree with her on all of it. From the looks on a couple of these deputies' faces, they agree with her, too.

Jack heaves with anger. It's a good thing Lily's working at the bakery today and not here to see him like this. He doesn't relax even the slightest. Mack's on the phone to the club's lawyers. He hops in the truck with Worley. They follow the car carrying Nanny.

"Come on, Jack. Let's get to the station." We rush out to my truck. Jay jumps in the back seat.

Nick sends out an emergency alert. Before we reach town, every Viking within driving distance will be on their way to the Den. Granddad and Pops will fill them in. This is bad. I'm not sure how much more the McLeods can take. Hopefully, the lawyers will have Nanny and Lil Mama out in a few hours. If not, every Viking and our friends will be camping at the Sheriff's Office, even if we have to sleep in our cars.

19
Coty

To say this day has gone from bad to worse is putting it mildly. Never in a million years would I believe Evelyn McLeod would be arrested, especially not for assault and battery. What a joke. Yes, she threw the candleholder at the preacher's wife—a candleholder of all things. I was there. I saw it. If that hit actually hurt the woman, Ms. Rhodes needs to be in a bubble-wrapped house and never allowed to leave. Heaven forbid if she ever stubs her toe.

If social media hadn't gotten behind this and hyped it up, this would have blown over in a week or two. Okay. Maybe a month or two. All right, probably never, but it would have been contained in our little town. Nobody would've been arrested for darn sure.

Jack's out of the truck before I have it in park. Mack is already halfway to the car, carrying his wife. Six more cars of our club members pull in behind us. Bankz is waiting by the front doors. He rushes to the car carrying his mother. Big Papa has to grab Bankz and hold him back before he gets arrested, too. It's obvious which parent Bankz gets his attitude from.

My club brothers and our family members shout their disapproval at Sheriff Bowers and his deputies when they step out of their cars. Nanny shakes her head at her husband and son. Lil Mama is yelling. Not that we can hear her through the closed window.

Sheriff Bowers motions for Mack to meet him at the back of his patrol car. "Settle your people down. I don't want to arrest anyone else."

"You shouldn't have arrested her." Mack heaves with anger.

"Jacob, calm them down. I won't ask again." Sheriff Bowers lowers his voice. "This is what they want. Don't give it to them."

Jack steps in front of his dad and glares down at the Sheriff. "You arresting her like this is giving them what they want." He slowly shakes his head. "You're no better than the rest of them."

"Rodeo," Mack calls out.

"Jack, easy man." I take his arm and pull him away. He's in shock, or I wouldn't have been able to move him otherwise. "We need to help Worley settle everyone down."

"You help him." Jack jerks his arm away. He storms to the front doors and waits for his mother. I let him go. I get it. I don't know how I'd act if this were my mom.

Hendrix grabs Bankz from behind and squeezes tightly. "Shut up! You're not helping her."

Bankz doesn't listen. The moment Lil Mama's out of the car, he starts again. "These pigs need to let my Mama go!"

"Jerrad." Big Papa gets in front of him and points his finger in his son's face. "You settle down. If you don't, Hendrix is taking you out of here."

"But…"

"Jerrad," Big Papa warns.

Bankz heaves several deep breaths and looks as though he might explode. He nods once to his father and thankfully keeps his mouth shut.

"We're going to walk in here. You can stomp if you need to. You can glare holes into every cop in this building, but you're gonna stay quiet. Got it?" Hendrix lays it out for his best friend. He doesn't release Bankz until he nods that he understands.

Mack follows close behind Nanny as Sheriff Bowers escorts her into the Sheriff's Office. Bankz runs to catch up with his dad, and they walk in behind Lil Mama.

"Jay." I nudge his left arm with my elbow and glance down at his right hand.

Without a word or any sign that he heard me, Jay closes the knife and slips it into his pocket. I'm gonna need help. There's no way I can keep Jack and Jay both under control. Maybe I should stick close to Jay. Jack's got his dad. Jay's a loner. Always has been.

"I got him." Cloudy Daze comes out of nowhere. He tosses an arm over Jay's shoulders. "Come on, Blade. Let's go in here and listen to these not-so-wonderful men in uniform spew out a bunch of nonsense. Idiots. The whole lot of them."

Jay still doesn't speak. At least he listens to Cloudy and quietly walks into the Sheriff's Office. With Jay taken care of, I can keep an eye on Jack so our Prez can be there for his wife.

Worley and I pause at the door and face the rest of our family. "Vikings, go home, to work, or to the Den. We'll take care of this and have Nanny and Lil Mama home as quickly as possible." He points and moves his arm to gesture to all of them. "But don't any of you do anything. Don't retaliate. Church at six. Dinner after."

They all grumble and look defeated. I know how they feel. Everyone gets in their cars and leaves without any more problems. Townsfolk watch from across the street with their phone held up. Great. Social media will have a field day with this.

I look up at Worley. "You alright, man?"

He presses his lips together and takes a couple of deep breaths before meeting my eyes. "I just watched my club Queen, my best friend's ole' lady, walk into this building in handcuffs. No, Rodeo. I'm not alright. I'm pissed. I never want to see anything like this again." He turns, about jerks the door from its hinges, and storms inside.

I follow him in, expecting our brothers to be halfway calm. It's a hope quickly dashed. The room is in total chaos.

Mack jabs his finger at Sheriff Bowers when they try to take Nanny behind the counter. "Don't put my wife in a cell, Nathan!"

"She's under arrest, Jacob. She has to be booked," Sheriff Bowers says.

"Book her, but no cell," Mack demands.

"Put me in a cell!" Lil Mama yells.

"Dar, hush," Nanny pleads.

"Nope. Lock me up!" Lil Mama gets louder. "Lock me up!"

Sheriff Bowers closes his eyes and takes a deep breath. He nods to the two deputies holding Lil Mama's arms. "Book her, and put her in a cell."

The deputies nod and carry Lil Mama back to the booking area.

Bankz goes insane and rushes toward the counter. "Don't you dare!"

Hendrix grabs him from behind again and literally drags him outside. Big Papa even holds the door open for them. The out-of-hand Viking is out of the building.

"Look." Worley walks up to the counter. The female officer at the desk glares up at him. He pays her no mind and focuses on the Sheriff. "Our lawyer will be here in less than twenty minutes. Book 'em. Put 'em in an interrogation room. We'll post bail and take 'em home."

"I'll see what I can do." Sheriff Bowers nods.

The front door flies open. A woman with long brown hair in a fancy business suit rushes to the counter. Pretty. Never seen her before.

"See that you handle things in a timely manner, Sheriff." She adjusts her purse strap on her shoulder. "Judge Simmons just set bail for Mrs. McLeod and Mrs. Banks. Get the paperwork ready, and I'd like to see my clients."

I glance at the others. They're doing the same. No one knows this woman, but she seems to be on our side.

"And who are you?" Sheriff Bowers is as confused as we are.

"Oh." She pulls out a fancy business card and hands it to him. "I'm Ciara Hollis, attorney for the McLeod family."

"Hollis?" Sheriff Bowers stares at her in disbelief.

We're all shocked. Robert Hollis is Granddad's friend. Robert moved his firm to Nashville thirty years ago. His firm has always represented the Viking Warriors.

"Yes, and I want to see my clients. Their bail was set at ten thousand each. The bail bondsman is on the way." She doesn't wait for Nathan to respond. She walks up to Mack and extends her hand. "Hello, Mr. McLeod. I apologize for meeting like this. I was closer to Willow Creek than Ben Fowler was. My grandfather called and said this was urgent. I got here as quickly as I could."

"We're glad you're here." Mack shakes her hand. "Don't let them put my wife in a cell. Her mind can't handle those bars closing on her. Enough closes on her already."

Miss Hollis tilts her head slightly and dips her chin in a classy little move. Didn't know that was possible. "Don't worry, I'll have your wife and her friend out of here within an hour." She shrugs one shoulder and grins. "Half of that with my witty charm." She smiles at the rest of us before walking behind the counter. "My clients, Sheriff."

"Your client assaulted the preacher's wife," Morine Johnson, the female officer at the desk, mumbles.

Miss Hollis stops even with the desk and glares down at Morine. "Your preacher's wife harassed and provoked a grieving mother on the day of her daughter's death. Not cool. Not kind. I won't tolerate it." Miss Hollis lifts her chin and walks past the Sheriff. "If I don't see my clients in the next three minutes, Sheriff, I'm calling the Judge."

"Where has Robert been hiding her?" Worley asks.

"No clue." Mack smiles. "But I'm calling him when we're out of here and thanking him."

20
Kayla

Kira was thrilled when I showed up a day early. The four-hour drive took closer to five hours. I was in such a hurry to get out of Willow Creek that I didn't eat breakfast. I stopped an hour into the drive for gas and food, and once more for a light lunch.

The first night, we chilled out at her apartment and ordered pizza. Kira slipped into her room to take a call from her fiancé. She wasn't the same when she returned to finish watching a movie with me. She hardly spoke the rest of the night.

For two days, we've been all over Knoxville and a few of the surrounding towns in search of wedding supplies. As I suspected, this wedding is being thrown together on short notice. It's like she woke up a week ago and said *Hey, I'm getting married in two weeks.*

We've been to discount stores, thrift stores, and a local used clothing boutique that one of her neighbors owns. It's where we got our dresses. They're pretty, but none of the discount stores had a dress in her price range that could substitute as a wedding gown. Naturally, my dress is purple, her favorite color. She promises to have them dry cleaned before next weekend. I'm all for being thrifty or frugal, but this is ridiculous. I mean, her two-tier wedding cake is coming from *Walmart*.

I see so many red flags about this. Maybe I'm more aware of a few things because I help with Ariel's Angels. One thing really bugs me.

"Hey, Kira."

We're staying in again tonight. I was supposed to have left yesterday. Since I don't have to work until Friday night, I figured one more night wouldn't hurt. And I'm avoiding Coty. It's not like he's called or texted me in the last three days. It kinda hurts that he listened when I told him to stay away.

"Yeah." She sets our Chinese containers on the table.

I grab my orange chicken and rice and follow her to the couch. She's avoided talking seriously with me. I'm leaving in the morning, so I need some answers.

"Why haven't I met your fiancé? And what's his name?" She calls him C. C. when he calls. You'd think the man would be eager to meet his fiancée's friend.

"Oh, he works in North Carolina through the week and only comes home on the weekends."

Okay. I get that, but something's wrong. She's not comfortable talking about her boyfriend.

"And his name?" This should be an easy one for her.

"Um." She huffs out a breath that pushes the loose strands of hair from her face. "Cory Coleman."

Now, I'm a different person. Cory Coleman was friends with Trent Colby. I'm not sure if they're still friends. They must be, or she wouldn't act so weird when talking about her boyfriend with me. My guess is that Trent will be at the wedding. She didn't date Cory in college. She hasn't told me how they met. Cory and Trent weren't best friends in school. Still, they were close enough that if I had known there was a possibility of Trent being at this wedding, I would have told Kira no.

"You should have told me." I set my food on the coffee table.

"I know. I'm sorry." She won't look at me.

"Trent will be there." It's not a question.

"Yeah," she whispers.

I should bail. It wasn't like she asked me to be her Maid of Honor. I was just appointed the position. She is my friend. Somehow, I'll figure out how to get through the wedding. Maybe I can get someone to come with me. Coty instantly pops to mind. If I talk to him and work things out, he'd come with me next weekend. Trent wouldn't come near me if Coty were there. But that means I'd have to tell Coty about my history with Trent. That's not something I want to talk about with anyone. Will Coty even speak to me after I disappeared for four days? And there's the fact that I pulled a gun on him. He would. I'm sure of it. Do I want to talk to him? Yeah, I do. I didn't handle things well on Monday morning. I was a total B to him.

I need to do something to get Kira and me out of this awkward moment. "I'll make coffee."

Her phone rings as I walk into the kitchen. "Hey, C. C., how's your night?" She's quiet for a moment. "What? You're what?"

Someone knocks loudly on the front door. An eerie feeling comes over me. Kira thinks nothing of it and rushes to the door. I pause, pouring the water into the coffee maker.

"C.C.!"

She sounds happy, so I go back to making the coffee. Well, I wanted to meet the fiancé. Now that he's here, I'd rather not.

"What? No. That's not true," Kira cries.

"You ungrateful piece of trash!" a man yells.

"No, Cory. Don't," Kira pleads.

What in the world is going on? The sound of a slap comes from the living room. Kira wails in pain. The slap comes again. That's not a hand. It's a belt. I knock the bag of coffee over on the counter in my haste to get to the living room. What I find horrifies me and pisses me off at the same time.

Cory has Kira trapped in a corner. She's crouched down on the floor with her arms over her head. Her cries and pleas don't faze him. He swings the belt back again, and I spring into action. I run across the room and cover Kira with my body. I cry out when the leather makes contact with my back. I nudge Kira to the side just before the belt strikes my back again. I hear my friend scream. Words don't register. I can't make out what they're saying. It's like I'm in a tunnel. All I feel is the sting of another strike.

Among Kira's screams, something crashes. Her screams stop, and she's there. "Kayla. Oh, Kayla. Are you okay?"

"Kira," I croak out her name and wince when she places her hand on my back.

"Sorry."

"Kira, what happened? Where is he?"

She takes my arm and carefully helps me to my feet. Her hand flies up to cover her mouth as she cries harder. "I think I killed him."

I'm scared to turn around, but I do. Cory is lying face down on the floor. There's blood on the carpet. A shattered lamp lies next to him.

"What do we do?" She wails louder.

I grab her shoulders and shake her hard. She snaps out of it for a moment.

"Go. Shove a couple of outfits into a bag. We're getting out of here."

"What about him?" She looks past me to Cory.

"We'll make an anonymous 911 call once we're on the road." I nudge her toward her room. "Go now. Only grab what you need, and fast."

Thankfully, she listens. I grab my things as quickly as I can. Within ten minutes, we're on the road to Willow Creek. An hour into the drive, I know I need help and make a call.

"Kayla, are you okay? Where have you been?" Lily asks.

"Nope, not okay. I need your help."

Lily shifts like she's sitting up. "Okay. What do you need?"

"We need a nurse." It's a good thing my friend is one. "Can you meet us at my apartment?"

"I can't leave club property right now. You come to the guest house. I'll let the guard know you're on the way."

"Why can't you leave?" Yeah, Jack's protective, but this sounds like something more.

"I'll tell you when you get here."

"Okay. I need another favor."

"Sure."

"Have Nick call in a 911 tip for a domestic violence dispute." I give her Kira's address.

"Kayla, what happened? How bad is she hurt?"

"I'll explain when we get there. I'll see you in three hours." I pause and glance at Kira. "I'm bringing an angel with me.

21
Kayla

It's nearly midnight when we pull up to the gate at the Viking Warriors clubhouse. We only stopped once for gas and to grab some snacks. The tank is almost on empty, but I wanted to get here as fast as we could. And I admit, I'm worried about what happened in Kira's apartment. I didn't check to see if she really killed him or not.

Surprisingly, Hendrix is on duty at the guardhouse tonight. He hasn't pulled guard duty that I know of in years. Instead of immediately opening the gate, he walks out to my car.

"Kayla." He leans down and looks at Kira. She's slouched down low like she's trying to hide from the world.

"Hey, Ronin. We're meeting Lily at the guesthouse." I called Lily as we drove through town.

"Change of plans. Drive to the side entrance. Lily's waiting for you in Mack's office." Hendrix taps a finger on my open window.

"Yeah. Got it. We'll go to Mack's office."

Hendrix walks back to the guardhouse and opens the gate. Patches, one of the prospects, runs through and takes over. Hendrix walks behind the car through the gate. I wouldn't have been able to drive around to the guesthouse if I wanted to. Jay's standing in the parking lot. He motions for me to go to the lot where they bring the angels into the clubhouse.

"Kayla, what's happening?" Kira twists around to look through the back window. Jay and Hendrix walk behind us until I park. "You said we were meeting your friend."

"We are. She's waiting for us in the President's office."

"Is this normal? Who are these men?" She watches Jay and Hendrix walk to the side door. It opens, and Worley steps out.

This isn't normal. Well, maybe it is. I've never delivered an angel before.

"These men are trusted club members. They're here to help us. I promise." She's my friend, but I'm not supposed to tell anyone about Ariel's Angels. That's Mack and Nanny's job.

I should have texted Lily that I was bringing an angel when we stopped for gas. Kira has asked me about it at least ten times. When Mack and Nanny asked me to help with Ariel's Angels, I promised to never talk about their secret organization with anyone outside the club. I hope my little slip tonight and bringing Kira here doesn't break my promise.

Worley opens my door. All the Vikings give Kira space. They stay close, but not too close. "Kayla, welcome home. Lily's waiting for you in Mack's office. We'll talk with your friend after."

"Thanks, Worley." I hurry around and open Kira's door before she has a full-blown panic attack. She immediately latches onto my arm. "It's gonna be okay. I promise."

Jay stands next to the side door. "You're safe here, angel," he assures Kira and goes back to watching the parking lot.

Worley leads the way down the hall. He opens the door to Mack's office and motions for us to enter. "Lily will let us know when you're finished."

Surprisingly, Lily's alone in Mack's office. She stands from one of the leather chairs on this side of the desk. A black doctor's bag sits on the desk. That's new. Lily used to be a nurse in LA. Hopefully, this is a sign she's ready to step back into the medical field. Her skills and training are wasted working at the bakery.

"Kayla, who do we have here?" Lily smiles sweetly at Kira.

"This is my friend, Kira Mitchell. We were roommates in college."

"I don't understand, Kayla. This is all weird. I should go home." Kira turns towards the door.

"No," Lily and I say at the same time.

My eyes meet Lily's, and I instantly know something more has happened.

"I don't belong here. I shouldn't have come," Kira tries for the door again.

"You don't belong in Knoxville, either." Lily's words cause Kira to pause at the door.

I walk over and gently place my hand over hers on the doorknob. "I know it's all a little scary right now, but trust me. They can help. I wouldn't have brought you here if I weren't sure of it."

"They helped me," Lily speaks in a soft, even tone. She's come a long way since meeting Jack. "And Kayla's right. We can help you. You won't have to go back to an abusive relationship."

"How can you help?" Kira lets go of the doorknob.

"First, I'm going to treat your injuries and decide if you need to see a doctor. Then, we'll talk about your situation with Jacob."

Kira's eyes bounce between Lily and me. "Who's Jacob?"

"He's in charge and will explain everything. If you decide you want our help, we'll start your journey to a better life." Lily motions to one of the leather chairs. "I'm a nurse. If you'll sit and show me your injuries, I'll take care of them."

"Okay, but I don't need a doctor."

Wow. Lily's starting to step into her role as the future Queen of this club. I'm so proud of her. Jack's a good influence on her. He can be a bad one, too, but in a good way. Lily will never complain about that side of Jack. More than half the women in this town secretly have a crush on him. It warms my heart to see her so happy. She's a woman in love and not ashamed to show it.

Kira sits on the edge of the chair. She lays her jacket on the seat and pushes up her sleeve. Lily moves a straight chair between Kira and the desk. She sits and pulls medical supplies from the black bag.

"I'm going to clean these marks and apply an ointment. It will help with the pain and the healing process. The skin is red, raised, and a little swollen. I have ice packs and some ibuprofen. It'll also help with any pain you may have." Lily follows the marks on Kira's right arm. "These marks are…" She pauses and looks Kira in the eye.

"From a belt," Kira replies softly to the unspoken question.

Lily goes back to treating the wounds. "Okay. Do you have marks or injuries in more places?"

"Um." Kira glances at me. I slightly shake my head. Lily notices but remains quiet. "Maybe on my back. I'm not sure. He pushed me into the corner and took off his belt. I dropped to the floor and covered my head."

A light knock comes on the door, startling Kira and me. Lily doesn't flinch or look up.

"That should be Nanny," Lily says.

I ease over and slightly open the door. Sure enough, it's Jack's mother.

"Hi, Kayla. May I come in?" She's not really asking.

"Yes, ma'am." I step aside and let her enter. Refusing the club's Queen would get me kicked out and banned quickly.

Mack, Worley, Jack, Jay, and Hendrix line the wall, waiting to speak to Kira. I close the door when Coty walks around the corner. Of course, he's here. Coty usually goes everywhere Jack does. Jack's little journey around the country is why Coty left Willow Creek for two years.

"Hello, angel." Nanny sits in the leather chair beside Kira. "I'm Evelyn. You can call me Nanny. Everyone else does. After Lily finishes, we'll talk about your situation."

Thankfully, most of Kira's injuries are on her arms from where she blocked the blows. Lily had her remove her shirt to be sure they treated all her injuries. My heart broke when we saw the old bruises and marks on her back and ribs. I turned away and pressed my fingers to my mouth so Kira wouldn't see me cry. Tonight wasn't the first time he's hurt her.

"How far along are you?" Lily asks as Kira puts her shirt back on.

Kira freezes and glances at me. I knew it. I asked several times, but she wouldn't admit it.

"About seven or eight weeks." Kira drops her head.

Lily presses her lips together and nods. She turns to Nanny. "I don't sense any signs of distress, but she should probably have an ultrasound to make sure everything is okay."

"Very well. We can arrange that." Nanny takes Kira's hand and lightly squeezes it. "We're here to help you and your baby."

Lily closes the doctor's bag and rushes over to me. "I'm so glad you're back." Before I can stop her, she throws her arms around me.

I wince and cry out. "Oh, no," I whisper.

"Kayla?" Nanny's voice is full of concern.

"What happened?" Lily moves behind me and lifts my shirt.

"No, Lily. Stop."

"No, ma'am." Lily refuses to let go of my shirt.

"You should treat her, too," Kira says. "She covered me so I could get out of the corner. He hit her several times before I grabbed the lamp."

"What?" Nanny exclaims.

"Sit," Lily orders.

I do as I'm told. Nanny and Lily gasp when they see the belt marks on my back. By their reaction, it must look bad. I know he hit me three times, maybe four.

"Things just changed." Nanny rushes to the door.

"No. Don't," I cry.

"Oh, I most definitely am." Nanny jerks the door open. "Mack, Rodeo, you need to see this."

"No!" I scream. Not him. Not Coty.

Both men rush into the office. Coty roars like I've never heard before and storms out of the room.

"Jack, Hendrix, go after him," Mack orders.

Lily kneels in front of me. "Don't worry. They'll stop him."

"Lily, my life is such a mess. I messed up. I…"

She covers my hand with hers. "I know."

"You know?"

She tilts her head and smiles lovingly at me. She's been around Nanny a lot. "A little, but not everything." She wipes a tear from my cheek. "But all's not lost. It's fixable."

I swallow hard and nod. I lean forward and let my friend treat my wounds. Is she right, though? Are things with Coty fixable?

22
Coty

I have never wanted to kill somebody before. The police guarding Cory Coleman in a Knoxville hospital won't save him tonight. I storm through the Den and out the front door. Before I can jerk my truck door open, a body slams into my back hard, pinning me to the closed door.

"Get off me!" I fight, but can't break free. Not a position to be in.

"Nope. Not happening." Jack uses all his weight to hold me against the side of my truck. Fighting him is pointless. I could never beat him.

"He hurt her. He's gonna pay."

"Yeah, he will." Jack doesn't ease up. "We'll get him, but we don't have all the details."

Has he lost his mind? "Her back is all the details we need!"

"Not true." Hendrix leans his side against my truck and lays his arm on the hood. He watches Jack and me like this is perfectly normal. "We don't know if Cory Coleman attacked both of them, and if there was another man involved. We wanna get the right man, or all of them."

Good point. But that's not helping right now. For four days, I went insane, not knowing where she was. No, I didn't listen when she told me not to stalk her. I camped out in her driveway. Even rode by her parents' house. Ran into her brother in town. David swore he didn't know where she was.

Nick called in an anonymous tip to the Knoxville police department after Kayla called Lily. Naturally, she and Nick told Jack, and they notified Mack right away. We held an emergency Church meeting with the members who were at the clubhouse tonight. There were enough of us here to handle things without calling everyone in this late.

"Kayla needs you." Jack's words hit me hard. I stop fighting. "Let's go back inside and find out what happened and who did it. We need to get Kayla and her friend settled and ensure they're protected for the night. They've been through enough tonight. We'll figure out what to do once they're taken care of."

"You're not stopping me?"

"No. We just need to handle it smart." Jack's the last person who would stop me. We all helped him when he went after the men responsible for hurting Lily.

"If there's more than one, he's still out there." Hendrix looks toward the road. No cars pass.

That's a creepy thought. Did someone follow them from Knoxville? All we know is the police found one man in Kira's apartment unconscious on the living room floor with a broken lamp next to him. It was easy to piece most of that scene together.

"Okay. You're both right. We need to know exactly what happened." I nod to Jack. He releases me, but stays behind me until we're back inside. Hey. I wouldn't trust me either.

Jack lightly taps on his father's office door. Jay lets us in. Mack's at his desk. Worley stands slightly behind him on his right. Nanny's on his left with her arm casually around his shoulders. Kayla and her friend sit in the two leather chairs in front of the desk. Lily stands behind Kayla's chair. Kayla briefly glances over her shoulder. She looks relieved to see us.

"Miss Mitchell, we're sorry for what you and Kayla went through," Nanny says.

I mentally kick myself. We missed hearing their story. We'll have to get it from Lily later. I highly doubt Kayla will talk to me.

"Miss Mitchell, I have to ask, do you want our help?" Mack leans forward with his elbows on the desk.

"What does that look like?" Kira asks.

"We help you get away from your abuser and help you start over," Nanny replies.

"But you have to follow the plan. There's no detouring from it," Mack adds.

Kira drops her head and lowers her voice. "Did I kill him?"

"You did not. Cory Coleman is under guard at a hospital in Knoxville. He has eight stitches in the back of his head and a concussion, but he will recover." Nick's in a chair behind Worley near the window. I didn't even see him at first.

"Miss Mitchell, was Cory alone?" Mack asks.

"Um." Kira looks at Kayla and then at Mack. "He was the only one in the apartment."

Kayla drops her head back and groans. What's that about? What are they hiding?

"It's important for us to know if someone else was involved." Worley senses she's holding back.

"I didn't see anyone else," Kayla says.

"But someone else was there?" Mack pushes for the truth. He already knows. We all do.

"I don't know where Cory's friend was tonight. They always come from North Carolina together on the weekends. He was going to be Cory's Best Man in the wedding." Kira sniffles and swipes at her cheek.

"What's this friend's name? I'll see if I can locate him." Nick's fingers hover over the keyboard.

"Trent Colby." Kayla shakes her head and glares at Kira from the corner of her eye. She knows this man. Something tells me he's more than just Cory's friend.

"It's been a long night. Miss Mitchell, do you want our help?" Mack asks again.

"What happens if I don't take your help?" Kira drops her eyes to the floor again.

Kayla reaches over and takes her hand. Nanny shakes her head at Kayla. She can't influence her friend's decision. This is something Kira must decide for herself.

"Then you're free to go," Mack replies. Kira's head snaps up. "Just never mention this conversation. Too many lives are at risk."

"How do I get home?" Kira looks at Kayla.

"We can get you a room at a hotel on the interstate. You can call someone to pick you up from there, or we can get you a bus ticket," Mack tells her.

Kira stares at Kayla for a long moment. Kayla doesn't move or offer to help her get back to Knoxville. I won't allow her to drive back into that city knowing someone there could hurt her again.

Kira drops her head again. "He'll kill me, won't he?"

"More than likely," Lily says softly. Her eyes meet Jack's.

Kira takes a deep breath and looks up at Nanny. "I don't wanna go back. Help me. Please help me."

Kayla, Lily, and Nanny go to Kira and wrap their arms around her. For a moment, I feared she'd return to Knoxville.

"Okay, Miss Mitchell." Mack stands after the ladies part. "Welcome to the Viking Warriors MC."

"And Ariel's Angels," Nanny adds.

"What's Ariel's Angels?" Kira asks.

"The organization that's going to save you and help you start over," Nanny explains.

"Okay. Let's get Miss Mitchell settled for the night," Mack says.

Nick looks up from his laptop. "A room at the Haven House is ready for her."

"What about Kayla?" Lily asks.

Mack and Nanny look at each other. Kayla starts to speak. Nope. She gets no say in this.

"She stays on club property." Everyone turns to me. "It's safer if she does."

"He's right," Jack agrees. "We don't know where Trent Colby is. If he was in the parking lot when the attack happened, he could have followed them here."

"She can have my room here. I can stay with my parents or at my grandparents' ranch if that helps." *I won't. I'm not letting Kayla out of my sight. No matter where she stays, I'll be close by.*

"Thank you, Rodeo, but that's not necessary." Nanny smiles sweetly at me before looking Kayla in the eye, daring her to dispute her decision. "Both ladies will stay at the Haven House until we have a better idea of what we're up against."

"That's an excellent idea," Lily quickly agrees. "I'll walk them up there."

Jack rushes forward. "Uh, angel. That might not be a good idea."

Lily lays her palm against his cheek and smiles. "It's okay, Jack. I know you hate going there. Jay or Rodeo can walk me back."

"That's not quite it." Jack huffs. "Well, it's part of it."

"What's the other part?" Lily tilts her head.

"Tell her now, Jack," Nanny insists.

Jack's shoulders drop. "Don't be angry."

"Wrong choice of words," Worley mumbles.

Lily takes a step back and pokes Jack in the chest. "Out with it, Jack."

"Nina's here," he finally just spits it out.

Lily blinks rapidly. "Nina? My friend, Nina Lowe? The woman who sent me here and saved my life is in Willow Creek?"

"She's the Haven House Mother," Nanny says.

"What?" Lily looks around the room. "How long has she been here?"

"We brought her back with us from LA." Jack reaches for her hand, but she holds it away from him.

"Nearly two months? My friend, I thought I'd never see again, has been here, on club property, for nearly two months."

Nobody moves or speaks. It's true.

"Why? Why wouldn't any of you tell me?" Lily asks, surprisingly calm.

Jack manages to catch her hand this time. "I'm sorry, love. Nina asked us not to tell you. She just made the decision to stay a few days ago."

Nanny nods, confirming it's true.

"Well." Lily pulls her hand away. She takes Kayla's hand and one of Kira's. "I'm taking these angels to the Haven House." She stops at the door. "Coty, Jay, Hendrix, follow us." She looks around the room. "I love all of you. I really do. Keeping this from me was wrong. I get why you did it. It's still wrong, though." She looks at Jack. "We'll talk when I get back. Right now, my friend is going to explain why she kept me in the dark."

Mack nods his approval. Jay, Hendrix, and I follow them to the Haven House. As much as I want to reach for Kayla, I don't. We'll talk tomorrow whether she's ready or not.

23
Kayla

Lily's hand tightens around mine as we walk up the steps to the Haven House. Jack refuses to go inside this house. Lily's only been to the kitchen through the back door a couple of times. This used to be Jack's house, their house. Their fear of this place is rooted deep. This is where Lily was shot.

"You don't have to do this."

Lily stands frozen on the porch and stares at the front door. The deep breath she takes lifts her shoulders. "I do. I want to see her." She glances at me and shakes her head. "I just won't go upstairs."

That's understandable. Returning to the place you almost died has to mess with a person mentally and emotionally. I'm not sure I could do it.

"Okay. You don't have to, and if at any time you need to leave, that's okay too." If I see any signs of a panic attack coming, I'll rush her outside.

Kira narrows her eyes. I give my head a little shake. I'll explain things to her later. Lily's focused on the door again and doesn't notice our silent conversation. The guys watch us closely. They'll step in and help if Lily needs them.

Coty

I wish Lily wouldn't do this tonight. We could have Nina meet her at the guesthouse or Mack's office in the morning. She's come a long way since waking up from her coma. She's getting stronger physically and mentally. She's finding the version of herself she lost while in an abusive relationship—an even better version than before. I've learned enough about her to know she won't turn back. She's doing this.

I raise my hand and knock on the door. The locks slowly disengage. The person on the other side is hesitant. Finally, the door opens.

Lily gasps, and her knees slightly buckle. The fight she had in Mack's office is gone. "Nina."

With tears running down her cheeks, Nina steps onto the porch and wraps Lily in her arms. "Oh, my sweet girl."

Kira and I release Lily's hands. She throws her arms around her friend, and they cry together. I wipe a fingertip under my eye. Lily's told me so much about Nina. It broke my heart to hear her talk about the friend she lost. I hated that I couldn't tell her Nina was here. Nina is one of the first women Jack's family rescued. I was too young back then to know what was happening. I was barely a teenager when Nina left town.

"Do you want to come in?" Nina holds Lily at arm's length.

"For a moment." Lily sniffles and nods. "Just to the living room," she quickly adds.

Nina puts an arm around Lily's waist and looks past us to Coty, Jay, and Hendrix. "Gentlemen, thank you for escorting these lovely ladies tonight."

"Not a problem," Hendrix assures her.

"Jay, sweetie, I'll call if we need you." Nina smiles lovingly at him.

"Rodeo, say goodnight." Nina turns to me. "Kayla, please show your friend inside. We'll get you ladies settled."

"Yes, ma'am." I take Kira's hand and pause in the doorway. Hendrix has moved to the middle of the yard. Coty and Jay still stand at the bottom of the steps. "Don't go far. Lily will need someone to walk her back."

My words mean more than that. I just can't bring myself to say more.

"Not about to leave her." Jay's been quieter tonight than normal. He and Jack are close., He doesn't need to be asked to stay. He wasn't going anywhere. A knife twists in my heart when my eyes meet Coty's. I hurt him. I hurt both of us. I find enough courage for more. "Will I see you tomorrow?"

"If you want to."

I nod. "I think I do."

"I'll be here, Sparky."

He's still calling me that horrid nickname. Maybe Lily's right. There just might be hope for us.

"Kayla, we need to go inside and close the door," Nina says.

She's right. It's past midnight. There's at least one angel in the house, and she has a little boy. A part of me wants to stay out here and try to talk with Coty. A bigger part of me is too broken and too afraid.

"I'm tired." Kira drops my hand and steps inside.

"Goodnight," I whisper and hurry into the house.

Nina closes the door and turns to hug Lily again. Kira stands at the edge of the living room. Her wide eyes take in everything. Fear and uncertainty of what's ahead show on her face. Lily stares in awe for a different reason.

The house is decorated beautifully. It's cozy and comfortable. No signs that this was once a bachelor's home exist anymore. The furniture, decorations, and the paint on the walls have all been changed. One corner of the living room was turned into a play area for the angels who have little ones. If children have their own little place, it helps the mothers feel more relaxed.

"You're safe here, Kira. There are only women in this house." Nina accepted the role of House Mother when Nanny came up with the idea of turning Jack's house into a home for the angels as they pass through Willow Creek.

"More women are here?" Kira bites her thumbnail. "Like me?"

"At times there are." As a trained professional, Nina detours the conversation. "Your room is ready if you want to go to bed. You and Kayla can even share a room if you'd like. You've come a long way. If you're hungry, we had lasagna for dinner."

Kira's hand drops to her stomach at the mention of food. My stomach feels those pains too. We got a burger and loaded up on snack food at the travel center. That was hours ago.

"Food sounds good. We've mostly had junk food." Kira looks too afraid to speak up, so I do. "I can help you fix it."

"We were eating dinner when…it happened," Kira says softly as she slides into a chair at the kitchen table.

"Road food is not the same." Lily gets glasses from the cabinet and pours us all some sweet tea.

Lily shares a little of her story with Kira while Nina warms up the leftover lasagna and garlic bread, and I cut up vegetables for a salad. Within twenty minutes, we have a meal. The conversation while we eat changes to lighter subjects. No mention of men or abuse. It really helps Kira to relax.

"So." Lily pushes her plate aside and leans forward with her forearms on the table. "Why didn't you want me to know you were here?"

Nina dabs her napkin to the corners of her mouth. "At first, I wasn't staying. I didn't want to put either of us through saying goodbye again."

Lily leans back. "Yeah. The first time was hard enough." She regains her composure and gives a quick little jab of her finger at Nina. "You could have explained all this better."

Nina laughs nervously. "I really couldn't. We all swore to keep the organization a secret. Only Jacob or the other chapter presidents explain things." She glances away and lowers her voice. "Not all the angels let us help them."

"This isn't legal, is it?" Kira's eyes shift between the three of us.

"Not exactly," I admit.

Nina takes over. She's better trained for this. "The McLeods tried working with the police to rescue women from domestic violence. There's a lot of red tape involved. We're just bypassing the red tape."

In other words, no, this isn't exactly legal. Women and children's lives are being saved. That's all that matters to me.

"Try not to worry and just rest tonight. Jacob will explain things when it's time." Nina gives Kira a reassuring smile.

"And when will he do that?" Kira lays her fork down and pushes her plate away. She ate more than half of her food.

"Probably Monday. The club gets busy on the weekends," Nina replies.

Kira's head snaps toward me. "Club? I don't want to go to a club?"

Nina taps her hand on the table, drawing Kira's attention. "You won't. You'll stay here with me." She changes things back to a calmer atmosphere. "If you're ready to get some sleep, Kayla will show you to your room."

Lily stands. "It's late. I should go so you three can go to bed. I'll help clean up first."

"Nonsense. I got this." Nina walks around the table and hugs Lily again. "I'm so glad you're here."

"You're really not leaving?" Lily's eyes well up with tears.

"I'm not leaving." Nina shakes her head. "My family's here. I have to be careful, but I don't want to leave them again."

"Can I see you tomorrow?"

"You come to the Haven House any time you want." Nina leans back and grins. "We can catch up. I want to hear all about how you, my friend, ended up with that sexy biker."

Lily lightly laughs. "Yeah, that happened."

It sure did. She not only ended up with a sexy biker but also the club president's son. There are a lot of broken hearts around Willow Creek. More than half of the women in this town dreamed of being with that man. Some of those women aren't even single.

"I'll walk you to the door. I'm sure at least two of those men are still waiting for you." Nina winks at me over her shoulder as they walk away. Coty's definitely one of those men. "Kayla, show Kira upstairs, please. I'll get the dishes."

Kira and I get our bags from where we dropped them on the couch. She trembles as we start up the stairs.

"Can we really share a room? I don't want to be alone."

"Sure." I lead the way to the last room on the left. It's across the hall from Jack and Lily's old room. That room has been turned into an office and storage rooms. This room has two twin beds.

While Kira changes, I go to the window and peek through the blinds. This room has a view of the front yard. I'm kinda glad Kira wanted to share a room. All three men waited for Lily. Jay and Hendrix walk down the path next to Lily, one on each side. Coty's behind her. As if sensing I'm watching, he pauses and looks up at the window. I don't run. I don't wave. I just watch. After a long moment, he dips his chin and hurries to catch up with the others.

Kira watches over my shoulder. "I wanna know how you ended up with that sexy biker."

"He's not mine," I whisper.

"Girl, you're blind and an idiot. He definitely is." She crawls into the bed furthest from the door.

I turn out the lamp between us and climb into the other bed. Coty's mine. Well, technically, he's not. Yet.

24
Kayla

Due to the fact that Kira is an official Ariel's Angel, she's not allowed to leave the Haven House. Nina wants to spend some time with her and see if she'll open up more without me around. It didn't hurt my feelings when Nina sent me to the clubhouse to help Nana cook breakfast. I felt Kira was holding back. Let's face it. She kept a lot from me while we were in Knoxville.

"Oh, Kayla. I'm glad you're here. Will you take some coffee out to Granddad and Pops for me?" Nana only looked away from the stove long enough to see who entered the kitchen. She's the only one here.

"Sure thing." I've always jumped in and helped where they need me. I grab the freshly brewed pot and go through the door to the bar. You can't get behind the bar from the Den side. It's a safety feature Granddad had installed years ago.

"Kayla." Pop calls out the moment he sees me. "Where you been hiding, girl?"

"I was in Knoxville for a few days." I refill his cup.

"Brought us back an angel, too." Granddad gives me a firm nod.

"That so?" Pop sounds shocked and impressed.

"It is." I move to Granddad's cup.

"Good job. Knew you'd be an excellent helper." Pops gives me a high five.

The people who work closely with the angels are referred to as helpers. Most of them handle transportation. A few, like Nina, have official titles. This was my first time transporting an angel. I understand now how Nina felt when she made the decision to save Lily. Knowing your friend is safe and alive is far better than letting them continue being abused or worse.

"Can I get you two anything else?"

"Food. I'm starving." Granddad takes a sip of coffee. He prefers his black.

Lily's laughter fills the Den as she and Jack enter the room from the hallway. Jack gives her a long kiss before she goes to the kitchen. Jack walks up to the bar and slaps his hand down.

"Morning, Kayla. I'll have a cup." Jack takes the stool between Pops and Granddad. "You sleep well?"

"Not bad, considering." I glance toward the hallway. It's rare for Jack's shadow not to be following him.

"He's not here." Jack takes the cream and sugar from Pops.

"What?" Playing dumb doesn't work this morning.

"Coty went to his grandparents' ranch. One of their ranch hands got hurt." Jack grins. "But we'll watch over you until he gets back."

"Uh." I storm back to the kitchen. "I don't need anybody watching over me," I grumble.

"Not true." Nana pulls a pan of biscuits from the oven. "There's a mighty big problem in Knoxville."

"What problem? Nick said Cory was going to be fine."

Lily grits her teeth as she scoops a large spoonful of scrambled eggs onto plates. "Cory will recover, but he's a problem. He told the cops you and Kira attacked him."

"What? No. That's not true."

"We know, but the police in Knoxville need proof." Lily sets the frying pan back on the stove. "After breakfast, we'll go to the office so I can take pictures of your back. Nina will document Kira's injuries. I'll give everything to Nick, and he'll create a medical file."

"Don't we need a doctor for that?"

"I'm a nurse. Close enough." Lily fits in perfectly here. She's becoming as sneaky as the rest of the McLeods.

"Do you wanna trade places with Dobbs and work at the Den tonight?" Nana pushes a tray of bacon in front of me.

"I really need the tips from the Roadhouse." I place four slices on each plate. Two slices will never do for a Viking.

"When does your shift start tonight?" Lily asks.

"At four. After breakfast, I need to go home." I cover the sheet pan with a new piece of parchment paper and line it with more bacon.

"Not without a prospect you don't," Nana informs me.

I spin around. "What? I don't need a prospect."

"It's the only way you're leaving here." Jack walks in. He kisses his grandmother's cheek before wrapping his arms around Lily from behind.

"Why? Because Coty said so?" I snap.

Nana slaps a spatula on the counter and points it at me. "Listen here, missy. Rodeo is a patched member. He'll be VP one day. He carries a lot of weight around here. Of course, we're gonna listen to him and take what he says seriously."

"But I'm not his ole' lady. He doesn't get to tell me what I can and can't do."

"If he hadn't left, you'd already be that boy's ole' lady. We all know it, you included." Nana starts another pot of coffee.

"He's not a boy," I mumble. It's the only comeback I have for her.

"Good. Glad you see it. Now, stop acting like some high school drama queen and treat him like a man." Nana doesn't tolerate nonsense. Guess she's tired of mine.

"Coty only left because of me. Sorry bout that," Jack apologizes.

"Coty did what any good friend would do." Nana pats Jack on the back. She comes to the opposite side of the counter and faces me. "But that ain't all that's itching your craw, is it?"

I lean back, unsure of what to really say. "Nana?"

"One, your parents are harsh people. Demanded things of you they shouldn't have. Not your fault." She gives a quick little point to me. "Two, you went off to college. Got tangled up with a man you shouldn't have. Now, you're bleeding on a man who never hurt you. You're blaming him for leaving. Your bad things aren't his fault."

"Nana, that's…"

"No, ma'am. I'm talking. You're listening." Nana doesn't wait for me to acknowledge her. "You didn't let Coty in when he tried to get close before he left." She motions to Jack over her shoulder with her thumb. "If you had, he may have talked this yahoo into coming home after a couple of months, not two years."

"That's not my fault."

"No," she agrees. "And what happened to you isn't Rodeo's fault. He's not the board you get to throw darts at because you can't throw 'em where they need to go. He's a safe place. He loves you. You've loved him longer." She slaps her palm on the counter. "Now, go make peace with it, and give that man the chance he deserves."

Nana turns around and goes back to cooking like she didn't just drop some truth bombs on me. What do I do with all that? Telling her she's wrong will get me tossed out of here and banned from the club forever. She's not wrong. I'm not sure how to process it, though. No one likes having the truth thrown at them.

"Thanks, Nana." I sigh in defeat. "I think I'll go home now."

"Patches is waiting for you," Jack says.

Fine. I roll my eyes, nod, and keep my mouth shut. I don't want a prospect following me around. It's better than being stuck here all day, though.

Sure enough, Patches is waiting by my car in his truck. I feel like a prisoner with him following me. Thankfully, he stays in his truck in the driveway while I go inside.

My apartment is dark and lonely. I used to think living on my own proved I was independent and successful. I preferred being by myself. After spending the week with Kira and last night at the Haven House, I'm not so sure I like being alone.

I go to the kitchen and grab a bottle of water from the fridge. I'll need to go to the grocery store tomorrow. My University of Tennessee coffee mug in the sink catches my eye. I don't remember leaving it there. I left in such a hurry on Monday. Maybe I had a cup before I left. I don't remember. Most of that morning is a blur to me. Oh, well. I need a shower.

My bedroom is exactly how I left it. A big mess. It's kind of like my life right now. The sheet Coty had wrapped around him is still on the floor. The comforter is on the bed, but it's not made. I really did leave a mess in here and in the bathroom. My fluffy cream colored towel is hanging over the shower rod. I usually hang my towel on the clothing rack behind the door. At least it's dry and not a damp, crumbled heap on the floor. It's my favorite towel. I'd hate to have to throw it away because it mildewed while I was gone.

I don't like a messy apartment. There's plenty of time to clean before I go to work. First, a nice, long, hot shower sounds like heaven.

25
Coty

Nothing I hoped for happened today. Absolutely nothing. My plans, which I should've never made, were to meet Kayla when she left the Haven House. Nina won't let a man inside unless it's an emergency, when an angel is here. With two, one with a little boy, and Kayla sort of being a third, it was pointless to even knock on the door.

My bad day started before my feet touched the floor. My phone rang out on the nightstand and started again by the time I grabbed it. Not a good sign. Dad was on his way to my grandparents' ranch. One of their ranch hands was thrown from a horse, and an ambulance was on the way. I expected my grandfather to be on the verge of a heart attack when I arrived. He cares deeply for his workers. Instead, I found him walking around the yard, shaking his head.

One thing's for sure. Lee Howell doesn't belong on a horse. He'd be better off working at one of the stores or shops around town. He's eighteen and said he knew how to ride and herd cattle. He knew nothing. If you can't ride and you can't herd cows, just say so. The herd was scattered between three pastures and down by the creek. It took us all day to round them up. Dolly, the sweetest horse on the ranch, had had enough of Lee and threw him, breaking his leg. The medical bills will fall on my family, but the boy will never set foot on C. Michaels Ranch again.

"Heads up." Hendrix nods toward the two men who just walked into JB's Roadhouse.

The only way to be near Kayla tonight was to trade places with Cole. He's helping out at the Den. I'm playing bouncer. I don't mind tossing a man out the door. I'll do it in a heartbeat. I just hate that it's an office job. With all the people coming and going tonight, I can't go to the bar and talk with Kayla anytime I want. At least, I can see her from here. It helps calm my nerves knowing she's safe.

"See 'em," I confirm.

The two men who creeped out Angie and several of her customers make their way through the crowd. They join two clean-cut younger men at a table halfway along the back wall. Hendrix and I narrow our eyes. He stands on one side of the front doors. I'm on the other. The two younger men narrow their eyes, too. The bigger, dark-haired man from Angie's speaks. We can't hear what's being said from here. The younger two men move to another table across the bar like they had been set on fire. Good. They aren't working with these guys.

"You wanna toss 'em out?"

"Not yet." Ronin types a message on his phone. "Nick can help watch them. Maybe he's ID'd them by now."

Nick sends back the names Willis Sanford and Adam Lang. They're from Alabama. It doesn't mean they're not friends with the Midnight Mavericks. Surprisingly, the Mavericks have been quiet this month. So far, Sanford and Lang are just sitting at a table, talking, and drinking beer. The only people they've creeped out here are the two men they took the table from.

"Jay knows 'em. Might want him here," I suggest.

Hendrix looks at me like I'm insane. Okay. I admit it. Our knife-loving Enforcer gets a bit unhinged at times. In a fight, you'll want Jay on your side.

"Fine, but if he goes Blade on these guys, you're handling him." Hendrix steps outside to make the call.

Parker's behind the bar with Kayla tonight. She looks happy. She laughs and carries on with the customers. It's an act. When there's a pause from making drinks, she nervously glances my way. Watching her flirt with the men, especially the college guys, ticks me off. She's mine. They need to move on. Parker has orders to step in if they get too friendly with her.

The only customer Kayla's genuine with is the woman who helped her the night Blake's friend crossed the line and touched her. Eliza, I think? Can't remember. I've seen her around town a few times, though.

After an hour, Willis and Adam, not very tough names by the way, walk out the door. I'm not sure if I'm relieved or disappointed they didn't cause any trouble. It makes no sense for two untrustworthy men to show up in Willow Creek on at least two occasions and not cause any trouble. I mean, it's great for our townsfolk. For those of us who are used to trouble, it's an eerie red flag.

"They wanted to be seen."

I nearly jump across the doorway to Hendrix's side. Hendrix chuckles. I growl. Jay's now standing in my spot. Please tell me no one videoed that.

"Where'd you come from?" If I were a braver man, I'd stab him for making me look like a fool.

"Over there." Jay points to the right corner of the bar.

Bankz has a stool there, a little further back from the others. The area has no lights above it. It's darker, so it goes unused and unnoticed most of the time. Bankz sits there when he wants to secretly monitor the room and be close at the same time. A lot can happen during a fight in the three minutes it takes to get from his office and the security monitors.

"How did you get in?" I haven't left the door since he was called.

"Bankz let me in the side entrance."

That fool and I are going to have to talk. If he's going to let the scariest Viking we have in, he needs to let us know. How am I supposed to control Jay if I don't know he's in the building? The answer is simple. I can't. It's impossible to control Jay when he's mad. Hendrix might be able to. Usually, Jack has to talk his cousin down.

"Why do you think they wanted to be seen?" Hendrix asks.

"They drank one beer, and Sanford got a text just before they left." Jay looks toward the bar and back at me. "I'm sure you've got Kayla."

I nod. "I'll take Patches and make a few laps around town. See if we can find out where they went and what they're up to."

Patches has been in the parking lot all evening. He's done a great job watching over Kayla for me today. He's proven his worth several times already. Pops really likes him. He'll have no trouble patching in this summer when his year's up.

I keep my distance from Kayla until closing time. She didn't used to be so skittish. Somehow, we gotta find a way around that. Her new friend is still here, but it's time for me to get my girl out of here.

"You want a drink?" Kayla asks when I sit next to the only person left at the bar. "It'll have to be a bottle. We've already washed the mugs and glasses."

There's a dishwasher in the back. A mug or glass wouldn't be a problem.

"Nope. I'll get one when we get home."

"Home?" The woman snaps her head toward Kayla. "You forget to tell me something?"

"We don't live together," Kayla assures her. She's sort of wrong.

"You are?" I want to be a hundred percent sure of this woman's name before I call her the wrong one. That never goes well. Women can hold a grudge forever if you get their name wrong.

"Eliza. We met before." Her smile is more than sweet.

Kayla loudly clears her throat.

"Don't worry, Sparky." I wink at her. "I don't fall for flirty women."

"I'm not jealous." She lifts her chin.

"Oh, darlin. It's the cutest thing I've seen all day," I tease.

"Oh, say that again." Eliza rests her chin in her palm.

"Stop it," Kayla orders and turns to me. "We don't live together."

"Maybe not, but you're stuck with me tonight. You're place or mine?"

"You live with your parents. I'm not going home with you." She crosses her arms.

I have a room at my parents' house and my grandparents' ranch. I've been staying in my room at the clubhouse since I've been back.

"Your place it is. Grab your coat, Sparky. Time to go." I walk back to my spot at the door and wait for her. She's not happy, but she gets her things.

26
Kayla

Great. Just great. Let me say for the record right now, I don't like this. Not that anybody's listening or recording. Of all the ridiculous things I've had to do today, this is the worst. Coty's following me home and staying the night. I storm to the back to get my purse and coat. I take a quick moment to call Lily.

"Hey, girl. How'd your shift go?"

"No. No small talk. No being nice. Coty's following me and staying the night."

"Um. Yeah." Lily goes quiet.

I drop my head back and groan. "It's club ordered. Isn't it?"

"It is," Jack confirms. Great. I'm on speaker. "Even if it weren't, he'd do it anyway."

"Can't I just stay with you tonight?" I whine to Lily.

"Um." She's not going to answer me.

"Nope," Jack answers. "I'm having a wild night with my ole' lady. I don't want her to be quiet."

Lily gasps. Not in a shocked way. She's a freak and turned on. Jack McLeod has ruined a perfectly good woman. I'm kind of jealous.

Coty

"But..."

"So, Sparky, you let him stay or you go to the Haven House," Jack says.

"I'm not an angel," I point out.

"You're still in danger. You're Rodeo's woman. So deal with it. Gotta go now. I need to chase my prey. She looks like she wants to play." Lily squeals, and the line goes dead.

"Ew." I shudder and slide my phone into the back pocket of my jeans. I could've gone my whole life without hearing that. I love them both, but Ew.

Coty's waiting by the door for me. It looks like everyone has left.

"Where's Eliza?"

"Parker's making sure she gets home." Coty opens the door and follows me out.

Hendrix locks the doors and gives a firm nod before disappearing into the bar. He and Bankz are always the last to leave.

Halfway across the parking lot, I huff out a breath through my nose. Naturally, he parked near my car. His truck is in the next row, directly behind my car.

"You could ride with me. We can pick your car up tomorrow."

"No." I unlock the door and get in. "Uh."

"What?" Coty quickly scans the parking lot for signs of trouble.

"Nothing." I put the key in the ignition and slide my seat forward a little. Short people problems. Gotta reach those pedals after all.

My heart pounds and my mind races on the way home. Every time the thought of the night we spent together comes to mind, I slam a lid on quickly. I can't force those thoughts away this time. He's staying with me tonight, and neither of us is drunk.

Coty pulls into the parking lot and parks next to me. Even if I wanted to run, there's no chance of slipping out on him while he's sleeping. He'll make sure of it. Besides, I have nowhere to go. Running and avoiding him end tonight.

Jack's grandmother's words have played on repeat in my mind today. It was all true. Every last bit of it. How she knew some of those things is a mystery. It's not important. I won't try to figure it out. This town loves to gossip. I'm sure everything my father said about me at Sunday dinner was all over town.

It would be nice to have a few days to think about everything Nana said and prepare what I should say to Coty. I'm not getting that luxury tonight. Truth be told, I've had it for far too long.

Ever the gentleman, Coty opens my door and offers me his hand. Once I'm out of the car, he doesn't release it. He hits the lock button and closes the door. A part of me wants to jerk my hand away. The part of me that's listening to Nana lets the warmth flow up my arm. Oh, there's literally warmth. It's not a cliché.

I set my purse on the table by the door and drop my keys into the wooden bowl. Coty takes our coats and puts them in the closet by the door.

"You want that beer now?" I go straight to the fridge because I sure need one.

"If you can drink one without getting drunk, sure." He moves in way too close behind me.

I reach in, grab two beers from the twelve, and pause.

"You okay?"

"Yeah." I turn and offer him one. "I usually keep a twelve-pack. Just forgot I bought a new one."

Coty twists the top off his and tosses it in the trash. He stares into the bin.

"Are you okay?" I tease.

He closes the lid and runs a hand over his mouth and chin. "I'm just going to ask, but don't get mad."

That's a sign you're usually going to get mad. Why in the world would my trash make me mad?

"Sure." I take a sip of beer and remain calm, as asked.

"You got a drinking problem?"

Way to get right to the point. I spew beer out and quickly reach for the dish towel hanging on the stove handle. "No. Why would you ask me that?"

"Oh, I don't know. Let's see. There's a bottle of whiskey on the counter. You were beyond drunk Sunday night. You don't remember buying a new twelve-pack, and there are six empty bottles in the trash."

Really? All of that's true, I guess.

"I don't count my trash, Coty." I walk past him to the living room.

"You've only been home for a day."

I sit on the couch and toss my hands up. "I guess I forgot to take the trash out before I went to Knoxville." I honestly don't remember. I know I didn't take it out today. "It's just trash. So, chill out or go home."

"Okay." He doesn't believe me, but lets it go.

"Oh." I stop him before he can join me on the couch and point to the recliner. "Will you hand me that blanket, please? I usually keep it on the back of the couch."

He lays the blanket over my lap and sits next to me, really close. "You said last night you wanted to see me today."

"I've seen you for the last eight hours." I grab the remote and flip to reruns of *Friends*. It's just background noise. Something I can pretend to be interested in. I couldn't care less what the episode is about.

"Don't do that," he says softly.

"Give the man the chance he deserves." Nana's words almost shout in my head.

"I didn't handle things well Monday morning."

"That's very true." He sets his beer on the end table. "Would you really have shot me?"

"No." I set my beer on the table next to me. I've no desire to drink tonight, especially with him in the house. "The safety was on."

He glances at me from the corner of his eye. "Is that the only reason?"

I lightly laugh. "No, Coty. It's not." I turn my head to meet his eyes. "I could never shoot you."

"Good to know."

His hazel eyes reach into my soul and tie a cord. This happened a lot when I was a love-struck teenage girl while he gave me riding lessons. Lessons my parents regret letting me take. I was thirteen when my dad took me to Coty's grandfather's ranch for riding lessons. Coty was seventeen. I was too young for him back then—just a speck of dust in his eye.

"You wanna tell me why you hate me? Why you run?"

"Wow. No buildup. No easing into it, huh?"

"Why waste time?" His eyes drop to my lips. "Foreplay is saved for far better things."

I swallow hard. "I don't hate you."

"Then why are you mad at me?" His voice remains low and calm.

"You left."

"Yeah. I had to. My best friend was drowning in pain, grief, and losing his mind. I couldn't let him go out there alone."

"You were gone for two years."

"We were. It was freeing. I watched Jack regain himself. I promised his family I'd stay by his side." His eyes drift away for a moment. "Didn't really have a reason to come home."

Nana was right. I didn't give him any hope that we could be together someday. I didn't call or text Coty after he left. I let him go.

"There's more." It's not a question. He knows there's more.

"Yeah, but can we talk about those on another day?"

"If you promise not to push me away, sure."

Time to be brave. "I promise," I whisper.

His eyes drop to my lips again. "You really don't remember?"

"Bits and pieces." Flashes of the night we spent together started coming while I was in Knoxville. Each one made me feel like an even bigger fool for how I acted. "And you? Do you remember?" He said that morning that he was drunk too.

He leans close. His lips almost touch mine. "Every glorious moment of it."

My lips slightly part. I gasp against his lips when they touch mine. Thoughts of pulling away are lost, too, so I don't. I happily lean into the kiss. Finally, after all these years, I kiss the man who was once the boy I fell in love with. It's perfect. Wonderful. I savor every movement of our lips together. The slide of his tongue across my bottom lip steals the last of my reserve. I moan, and his arms tighten around me.

I pull away ever so slightly. "Can we go to bed now?"

"Only if you promise to remember it this time."

I smile against his lips. "Every glorious moment of it."

27
Coty

Four in the morning is not a time to be startled awake, especially when you fell asleep less than an hour ago. My horrible day and stressful evening turned into a wonderful night. A night neither of us will forget anytime soon.

My eyes quickly adjust to the darkness. Kayla is sleeping peacefully next to me. I hate to move and leave the warmth of her body. Something has the neighborhood dogs riled up. It's probably nothing, but I need to check it out just in case. I softly press my lips to her forehead and slide out of bed. I grab my jeans and t-shirt from the floor and quickly slide them on.

Kayla's apartment complex has three rows of one-story buildings. She lives in the last row. Houses sit on each side with a row of trees separating the yards from the apartment property. A wooden fence is along the back to hide the subdivision on the other side.

I peek through the blinds in the bedroom. The street lights are on, but I don't see anything moving. I slip to the living room and kitchen to look from those windows. Nothing. It can't be normal for this many dogs to be barking this time of morning.

I slowly open the front door. With one foot out on the concrete slab, I lean back against the doorframe. The barking is louder. Dogs inside the apartment next door and across from us bark, and probably even more. Plus, the ones at the houses on both sides of the apartments and some from the subdivision are acting up, too. These animals aren't happy. This can't be normal.

"Coty?" Kayla walks out of the bedroom, rubbing her eyes.

"Does this happen often?"

Half asleep, she slides under my arm and lays her head against my chest. "Sometimes, but I've never heard this many at the same time."

I ease us back inside, close the door, and lock it. "Grab your phone. Check online to see if something happened in the area. I'll look out the back door. Whatever it is, it probably happened in the subdivision."

"I'm sure it's nothing. Just crazy dogs or maybe one of their puppies is missing, and the parents called for help."

Haha. Very funny. This is not a Disney movie about Dalmatians. My little sister loved that movie. Mary knew every bark. Our parents had to hide it at times just to get some peace.

She stands next to the bedroom doorway and smiles sleepily. She's beautiful standing there with her messy hair, and the look, if I dare say it, of love in her eyes. I drink in every inch of her from head to toe as I flip the outside back light on.

My favorite image of her changes to wide eyes and horror. Her blood-curdling scream pierces my soul as she drops to the floor. My head snaps toward the back door. Like the front one, it has a window in the top half. Nothing's there. I rush to her side and lift her off the floor.

"What happened?" I carry her to the bed.

She sits on the side. Her hand shakes as she points toward the kitchen. "A...man...outside the door."

That changes things. I quickly shove my feet into my boots and grab my Colt from under my cut on the chair.

"You sure?"

She nods wildly. "Yeah."

I point to the nightstand on her side of the bed. "Call for help and grab your gun."

She springs from the bed and grabs my arm. "Please don't go out there. Wait for help."

As much as I want to go after this guy, I grant her wish. "I won't go out unless I have to." I give her a quick kiss. "Now, get your gun."

She opens the drawer and sucks in a breath. "Coty, it's not here."

"Check the other nightstand."

She hurries around the bed and opens the drawer. She straightens and slowly turns to face me. "It's not here." She covers her mouth with her hand. "This is bad."

This is beyond bad. I don't know where she got the gun. If it was by legal means, she'll have to report it stolen.

"We need help." I grab my phone and make the call.

"Rodeo?" Jack answers groggily.

"Ghost, I need the Vikings. As many as you can get."

"Where?" He's instantly awake.

"Kayla's apartment."

"What's wrong?" Lily's voice is heavy with sleep.

"Rodeo needs help. Call Nick." Jack puts his phone on speaker while he gets dressed. "Talk to me, Coty."

"Neighborhood dogs woke me up. Kayla saw a man in the window when I turned the back light on." I pause and meet Kayla's scared eyes. "And Kayla's twenty-two is missing."

"He's been inside."

"Is Kayla alright?" Lily's voice is full of panic.

Jack takes the phone off speaker. He's running out the door. "Nick's been notified. The SOS signal went out. At least a dozen Vikings are on the way. Jay's here. We'll be there in ten. Do either of you need medical?"

"No. There was no contact."

"Jack," Lily pleads.

"Sorry, angel. Back inside. You're staying here. Kayla's fine. We'll bring her to you."

The sirens in the distance destroy any hope of getting out of here without the cops being called. Vikings are not their favorite people right now.

"We have company."

"Yeah, I hear 'em. Just tell them what you told me. Looks like Hendrix will reach you first. Almost there, buddy." Jack ends the call.

I pull Kayla into my arms. "This isn't me being controlling, Sparky. But this changes things. You're not safe here. Pack a couple of bags right quick. We're moving you to the club property."

She leans back. Before she can protest, I crash my mouth to hers.

"Rodeo!" Hendrix pounds on the front door.

I slowly pull my lips from hers. "I can't lose you. I need to know you're safe at all times, especially while you're sleeping. Jack…" I run my hand through my hair. I can't finish it.

Recognition hits her hard in the chest. The thought ripped mine in two.

Kayla nods. "Ariel. Ariel was sleeping." She doesn't fight or protest. She grabs two suitcases from the closet and starts shoving clothes inside.

"Rodeo!" Hendrix pounds harder.

I rush to the door and jerk it open before he decides to break the glass. "We're good, man."

He nods toward the Sheriff's cars pulling in. "That's not good."

Kayla's apartment is the second one from the end. The couple in the first apartment opens their door when the cops show up.

Dennis Felton looks toward Hendrix and me. "Is Miss Kayla okay? A man ran across the backyard." Guess we know who called the cops.

"We saw him. She's shaken up, but okay."

Sheriff Bowers looks straight at me when Jack and the others pull in. Yeah, it's always the Vikings' fault when something happens around here.

"Get her stuff. I'll talk to Nathan. We'll move Kayla to the Haven House until this is over." Jack walks over to the Sheriff.

Kayla and I will briefly tell him what we know and get out of here. If they need more, they can contact us tomorrow. I want Kayla where I know she's protected, on club property. No one, not even the cops, can protect her like my brothers and I can.

28 Coty

It's just after five am, and the Den is filled with Vikings. It's not like Friday and Saturday night parties. We let the public into those. They get ID'd at the gate, and Nick runs a quick background search on them. Anyone we don't want on club property doesn't get in.

"Vikings!" Mack enters the Den. "Church!"

Surprisingly, Nanny and Nana walk in behind the Prez and Granddad. Even more surprising, Maci and my sister Ember are with them. Ember rushes across the room. I hold my arm out, and she wraps an arm around my waist for a hug. Kayla's tucked under my left arm.

"You two okay?" Ember sighs with relief just from seeing us.

"We're good. He didn't get near her." I'm not relieved. Anger grows within me every time I think about this man being inside Kayla's apartment. "Where's Mary?"

"She's at the main house with Everly."

"Alone?" The girls are seventeen. I don't want a prospect watching them unless there's no other choice.

"No. Jay's mother is with them." Ember smiles at Kayla. "Does this mean you two finally worked things out?"

"It's a start." Kayla looks up at me and presses her lips together.

I kiss the top of her head. "It's a great start, Sparky." My club brothers file into church. "I gotta go." I kiss the top of my sister's head, too. "Will you stay with Kayla for me?"

"Absolutely." Ember grabs Kayla's hand. "Come on, Lala. You can help us fix breakfast for all these Vikings."

"Lala?" Kayla glances at me and back at my sister. "You remember that?"

"Yeah. Mary still calls you Lala, and we do around the house. You're only Kayla to the rest of the world. To us, you're Lala or Sparky." Ember points at me as she pulls Kayla away. "One of those names goes on her cut when you claim her, not Kayla."

"What?" Kayla's eyes widen.

"Oh, can it, Lala. You know it's happening. Probably dreamed about it." Ember smiles, waves at me, and pulls Kayla into the kitchen.

Once everyone's inside church, Worley closes the door and takes his place down front next to Mack. I join Jack in the front row. It's weird and yet satisfying seeing Jay upfront with the officers. Our new Enforcer looks great up there.

"Okay, Vikings." Mack taps the gavel. "We have an emergency situation. As you all know by now, Kayla Chambers' apartment was targeted this morning. Her neighbors also spotted the guy and called the cops."

More than half the room groans. Others shake their heads. Even though the Viking Warriors MC is a clean, legit club, cops give us a hard time. It's crazy. There are hundreds of Christian clubs out there, and several clubs whose members are all police officers.

Worley takes over. "We're all patched members here. You've heard by now that Kayla brought an angel with her from Knoxville. Kayla and her friend, Kira, experienced some abuse from Kira's fiancé. Nick is trying to handle the legal issues with the Knoxville Police Department. We'll sit down with Kira on Monday and talk next steps with her."

Nick stands from his table down front on the lower level. "I'm ninety-five percent sure the incident at Kayla's apartment is connected to what happened Thursday in Knoxville. I'm not sure if it's Cory Coleman. He was released from the hospital late yesterday evening and had time to drive to Willow Creek by four am. Or," Nick pauses. "It's possible Kayla's ex, Trent Colby, is involved. The two men are friends and may be working together."

"Prez?" Pops raises his hand. It's rare for him and Granddad to join us. Both are here this morning.

"Yeah?" Mack motions for Pops to continue.

"If an angel brought this to our door, should we really keep her here for two more days?"

Mack glances at Worley. Our VP nods. His dad has a good point. "Take a vote," Worley suggests.

"We can't move Kira Mitchell just yet," Nick interrupts.

"Why not?" Worley asks.

"I'm still working with the cops in Knoxville. We have to be careful with this case. They know she's here and can more than likely prove we've helped her at some point. Detective Hernandez wants a statement from Kayla and Kira. I explained they were the victims and not the attackers, like Coleman claimed. I told him that bringing the ladies back to Knoxville might put them in danger. After seeing the photos Lily and Nina took of their injuries, he agreed to let Sheriff Bowers take their statements. They have an appointment with the Sheriff this afternoon. When I get Detective Hernandez's response, then we decide the day to move Kira. I vote that we move Miss Mitchell as soon as possible."

The club officers slightly nod to each other. Mack looks out at the rest of us. "All in favor of following Nick's plan for Miss Mitchell?"

I don't look to see how many member raise their hands. It feels like a lot. There's no need to ask for those who oppose. Mack does it anyway. I stay neutral. Enough agreed with Nick's plan already. My heart hurts for Kayla. She'll have to say goodbye to her friend soon.

"Prez?" Bankz raises his hand. Mack nods. "Are we protecting Kayla or moving her, too?"

I jump to my feet. "She's not leaving."

Bankz raises an eyebrow. A few of my brothers snicker.

"Of course, we're going to protect Kayla," Worley says.

"That brings me to my question." Everyone turns to Jay, our newest officer. "Are we protecting Kayla Chambers as a club friend or as Rodeo's ole' lady?"

"Does it matter?" I snap.

"Yeah, it does." Mack's the one to answer. I shouldn't have yelled at an officer, even if he is one of my best friends. "Ole' ladies get more protection and rights within the club."

They do. I know it. I've seen it many times. We protect club friends when there's a threat against the club that could affect them, or when their lives are in danger because of us. If they call us for help, we show up. Their protection isn't consistent, though.

"She's mine. I claim her."

Jack lays a hand on my shoulder. "You don't have to. You know we'll protect her."

"I want to." My eyes meet his. "I should have before we left." I'm not trying to make him feel bad.

Jack takes a deep breath and nods. He stays by my side through the vote.

"Okay, Vikings. All in favor of Kayla Chambers being Rodeo's ole' lady?" Mack asks.

I keep my eyes on Jay. It's his fault we're taking this vote. He raises his hand. So do the other officers. I don't look at my club brothers. I don't want to know how they vote.

"Those opposed?" Mack waits. I still don't look.

"Congratulations, Rodeo." Mack gives me a firm nod. She's mine.

"You have a road name for her you want on her property cut?" Worley asks.

Ember's words echo in my head. "Lala." Sparky is my name for her. My brothers don't get to use that one.

"Uh, Prez? We have a problem." Nick clicks around on his keyboard. The large TV monitor behind the officers' table turns on with the security footage at the front gate. Two Sheriff cars wait outside. "Patches says they have some questions for us."

"Anyone getting arrested?" Mack asks.

"If they are, Sheriff Bowers isn't saying." Nick's right. Nathan wouldn't announce that bit of information until he was inside the gate.

"Let 'em in. Church dismissed." Mack taps the gavel.

Coty

The sight of the Sheriff's cars pulling through the gate makes my skin crawl. I'm still on edge because of what happened this morning. Maybe they have info for us. Only, it feels like something more.

29
Kayla

Helping Ember and the ladies in the McLeod family prepare breakfast is actually fun. For one, you never know what Jack's grandmother is going to say. Nana was already with Granddad when he started the club. She's seen a lot of crazy stuff. The stories of the things she's done are even crazier. Some of those incidents are why she's in charge of the club bunnies. She put a few in their place back in her younger days. They don't get anything over on her now, either.

"So." Lily leans over the prep counter across from me and wiggles her whole body. "You and Rodeo. We need *all* the details."

Ember lays one hand on my back and slaps the other on the counter in front of Lily. "No, my future Queen. We do not. They're finally together. Let's just celebrate that. I don't want to hear what my brother does naked."

"You're no fun," Lily pouts.

Ember glances over her shoulder. "Mace, you wanna hear what Jack does between the sheets?"

Maci shudders. "No. Absolutely not, especially not with my Mom and Grandmother here."

"Well, if he's like his father, I'll have more grandkids soon." Nanny doesn't look away from the pancakes.

"Mom," Naturally, Maci's appalled.

"Runs in the family," Nana adds. I knew that was coming.

"Nana, not helping, " Maci scolds. "You're all creeping me out. Change the subject."

"She's right." Nanny waves a finger between Lily and me. "You two can have a girls' night and discuss those things."

"Sounds good to me." Lily grins like a Cheshire cat. She wants details she's not getting.

Voices come from the Den. All the guys, except for Cloudy Daze and the prospects, went to church today.

"Sounds like we've got hungry men coming." Nana grabs plates from the cabinet.

I peek through the door that goes behind the bar. All the members stand behind Mack as a group, staring toward the front doors.

"That can't be good," I say.

The others take turns peeking over my shoulder.

"Not good at all." Nanny goes back to the stove.

"Nope. Last time, Mom got arrested," Maci says.

"What?" I spin around and let the door close. "When did Nanny get arrested?" As far as I know, Evelyn McLeod has never been arrested.

"Monday morning, while you were on your way to Knoxville," Nana replies.

"Lil Mama was arrested, too," Ember adds.

Now, that I can see. It's surprising the woman doesn't have a rap sheet a mile long. She's always threatening to stab someone or to *'shove her boot where the sun doesn't shine.'* I give my head a little shake. That's not a thought I want to keep in my head.

"Why?" My eyes meet Nanny's. The sadness in hers causes my heart to sink. It's because of the candlelight vigil. I'm sure of it.

Lily pats my arm as she walks by. "Let's just say the Rhodes family isn't happy."

The door to the Den opens, and Worley walks in. "Hey, ladies. Hate to interrupt, but will you all join us?"

"Exactly how it started on Monday." Nana flips the stove burners off.

We silently follow Worley Bird to the common room. Nana goes to Granddad, who's on his favorite barstool next to Pops. Nanny slowly walks to Mack. This has to be scary for her after being arrested like this five days ago. Mack eases her slightly behind him. Nanny wraps her arms around his waist.

Jack lays a hand on his mother's back. Lily slides under his right arm. Coty holds his out for me. I quickly take the comfort and protection he's offering and wrap my arms around his waist. Ember and Maci stand next to us, holding each other. I don't like this.

"Okay, Sheriff. We're all here," Mack says.

"Like I was saying, I have a few things to discuss with you." Sheriff Bowers looks at Coty and me. "Coty and Kayla, we're not sure if the suspect this morning was targeting Kayla or not. We'd like to ask you some more questions at the station later this afternoon. We're asking neighbors to check their home security cameras. Anything, no matter how small, could help us catch this guy."

In other words, they have nothing. It doesn't matter how sure you are that something happened, or who was involved. The cops won't believe you without hard proof. I can't prove this was Trent or Cory. A feeling deep in my gut says it is. Oh, and feelings? Forget about those. Cops couldn't care less about your feelings.

"Next, I'm going to need the whereabouts and alibis for all your club members." Sheriff Bowers' eyes lock with Mack's. "Especially your immediate family members."

"Why?" Mack demands.

"This morning, Matthew Rhodes was found badly beaten at Willow Park. We need to know where everyone was between two and four AM." Sheriff Bowers' eyes move over our group.

"We were sleeping. Woke up at four to a bunch of dogs barking and a man at the back door." Coty's half right. The Roadhouse closed at two. We'd barely fallen asleep by four.

"Will Matthew be okay?" Nanny asks.

The Sheriff's eyes soften when he speaks to her. "I can't give you his medical information, but he should recover. He managed to crawl to his car and dialed 911 before losing consciousness."

I softly gasp. So do the other ladies. We glance at each other. The men remain still and calm. I don't like Matthew, but I would never wish anything bad to happen to him.

"Sheriff, we'll all tell you where we were, but why don't you cut to the chase and drop the final foot?"

"Mack…"

"No, Nathan," Mack interrupts. "There's more. You and I both know it. So, spit out. If you're here to arrest one of us, do it. But I tell you this." Mack stands up straighter. I swear, every time he does this, he adds another two inches to his already six-foot-three height. "My wife, mother, daughter, granddaughter, and their friends were here on club property, in our homes, all night. You're not taking one of them."

"No one's getting arrested." The Sheriff reaches the pocket inside his coat and pulls out a long, folded piece of paper. He offers it to Mack. Our Prez doesn't take it. "This is an order of protection. The McLeod family, every member, and the Viking Warriors MC, every member, are restrained from going within fifty feet of the Rhodes family, every member."

"Fine by us." Mack still doesn't take the paper. He motions to the tables. "You and your deputies can have a seat and get everyone's whereabouts between two and four this morning. As for the McLeods, every member, we were home, on club property, and asleep." He turns and kisses Nanny's cheek. "Go finish breakfast, love."

"You already know where Kayla and I were. We left the Roadhouse at two and were startled awake at four. You were there by four-thirty. Ember was here with Maci." Coty nudges Ember, Maci, and me toward the kitchen. "Go help Nanny and Nana."

Lily lifts up on her toes and kisses Jack. She grabs my hand and pulls me with her to the kitchen. This is insane. When will this madness end?

30
Coty

We have walked on eggshells for the past week. Keeping the McLeod and Rhodes families apart hasn't been easy. It's hard when both families live in a town as small as ours. The newest member of our legal team, Ciara Hollis, petitioned the court and got the order limited to the six immediate family members in Pastor Rhodes' family. Due to the rough reputation of motorcycle clubs, the judge kept the order to the entire club.

"How's Lala?" Jack asks.

Most of the club members have started shortening her name. She thinks it's weird. I love it. I still haven't told her I claimed her.

"Still mad that we moved Kira, but on everything else, we're good." Even with all the legal matters and uncertainty going on, this has been one of the best weeks of my life.

My brothers and I met up at Angie's for lunch today. Angie put us at a large table in the back dining room to keep us away from the Pastor's friends. Oh, yeah. There are a few in the front dining area. They can keep glaring holes in us. We don't feel a thing.

"Nick find any leads on who beat up Matthew?" Hendrix asks.

"Nothing concrete, but we think Sanford and Lang did it," Jack replies.

That's what we all believe. Willis Sanford and Adam Lang were mighty interested in Matthew at Angie's a few weeks ago.

"I don't doubt it." Jay finishes off his sweet tea. "The last camera Nick could catch them on was from Mel's Quick Stop."

You have to pass Mel's to get to Willow Park from town. Willis and Lang left the Roadhouse that night around two. It's enough for us, but not for the cops.

Bankz pushes his empty plate away. "You know, with Valentine's Day this weekend, why don't you see if Lala wants to bartend at the Den instead of the Roadhouse?"

"You don't want my ole' lady working for you anymore?" I'm teasing, but I tilt my head, cracking my neck.

Bankz isn't fazed. The fool actually grins. "Not at all. Just thought with all the parties going on Friday night, people could slip around town unnoticed for a while. I mean, *the suspect*," he makes air quotations with his fingers, "hasn't been caught, she'd be safer at the clubhouse."

"Good point." She's been as happy as I have this week. It's good to know my brothers are looking out for her. "I'll bring it up tonight."

"She's probably in a loving mood since she's helping out at the bakery this week. Ask quick before it changes," Jack suggests. The rest of us laugh.

Lala is helping Lily and Emily out this week due to the extra Valentine's Day orders. This is the first year I've wanted to celebrate the holiday. It's kind of pointless when you're single.

"Did Kira get settled?" I ask Jack.

He takes a deep breath. "You know you can't share her location or new life with Lala."

"I know, but letting her know her friend is okay and safe would ease her mind." She asks me every day if I've heard anything about Kira.

"You can tell her that much, but not the rest." I nod. Jack continues, "Shep carried her to Arizona. From there, she was taken to Drew." Jack shakes his head. "I don't know where Drew housed her. Kira isn't happy, but she's safe."

"What happened to her ex?" Hendrix asks.

"He was arrested for domestic abuse. Bail was set, but no one's paid it. The judge agreed to let Kira testify via Zoom from a police station in California. Her location won't be disclosed." Jack leans back and glances toward the front counter.

"No, Angie. We want a party table in the back." Sherry Rhodes comes to an abrupt halt when she sees us.

"I'm sorry, Ms. Rhodes, but you have to sit in the front dining room," Angie says.

"No. Make them leave," Ms. Rhodes demands.

"They were here first." Angie motions to the large round table in the front dining room. "According to the restraining order, they stay. You can leave, or sit there."

Ms. Rhodes huffs. "You always take their side." She lifts her chin. "Just wait until everyone hears about this. You'll lose half your customers."

"If they're all snotty and rude, I couldn't care less. I'm following what the law says in this situation." Angie motions to the table again. "Now, Ms. Rhodes, would you like to sit there or leave?"

"Come on, Mom." Finley lays her hand on her mother's arm. "This table is fine."

"But it's not private." Ms. Rhodes glares at us.

Finley holds her hand out and looks at her mother with wide eyes. "Mom, that's insane. We're meeting a few ladies from church and talking about the Valentine's party Friday night. We have nothing to hide. We could have used the fellowship hall if we did."

Ms. Rhodes turns her glare on her daughter. "Fine, Finley. You just listen to your father. Those barbarians hurt your brother. Stay away from them."

Jay sits up straight and slides to the edge of his chair. Jack clamps a hand down on his cousin's shoulder.

"Don't," Jack orders, low and deep. "And put the knife away."

The rest of us glance down at Jay's hand. Not that we all can see it. Thankfully, Jack heard Jay open the knife.

Jay glares back at Ms. Rhodes just as hard as she glares at us. The Preacher's wife snaps her head toward the front dining area and stomps over to the table Angie suggested.

"Not very ladylike. Is she?" Bankz mumbles.

Finley sighs and gives us a sympathetic smile. She mouths the words *'I'm sorry.'* Each of us dips our chins to her. The Vikings Warriors will never hate Finley.

Jay turns back to our table and drops his head. "Her father and brother are the real problem."

Jack needs to find out what Jay's deep hatred for Matthew Rhodes is. Sooner or later, Jay's gonna lose control, and no one will be able to save the Preacher's son.

"Why don't we get back to work?" Jack pats Jay on the back a couple of times. "I'll grab Cloudy's to-go order. Hopefully, he hasn't set the shop on fire while we were gone."

Each of us drops a ten-dollar bill on the table for Angie and heads toward the door. Hendrix shoves Jay forward when he pauses a few feet into the front dining area. Jack grabs Cloudy's order and helps get his cousin to the parking lot.

"See you guys later." I toss my hand up and jump into my truck.

While they go back to work, I'll swing by the bakery to make sure my ole' lady is okay. My ole' lady. I can't help but chuckle. I might not be laughing when she finds out I claimed her. The odd text from Skip, the prospect watching the bakery, makes no sense. It's not even words. That's not good. I start the truck. I have to get to Kayla.

31
Kayla

Helping out at the Cupcake Cottage was never on my to-do list. I love Emily and Lily, but getting covered in flour and cake icing isn't my thing. Oddly enough, it's been fun. Weird, huh?

"So, do you and Rodeo have plans for Valentine's Day?" Lily wiggles her eyebrows at me like a crazy person.

She has hounded me endlessly for details about Coty and me. I've given her the highlights. Some of our moments, well, most of them, are just for me. All I can say is I've never felt so loved, and we've only been officially together for a week.

"Well, I have to work, but I'm sure we'll find something to do after." I duck my head and grin. I have lots of ideas we can do.

"Have you had any more problems at your apartment?" Emily asks.

"No." I fill another bag with icing. I have the easy job of using a large decorating tip to apply a quick swirl of icing on the cupcakes.

Coty's stayed with me every night this week. He has a prospect or a club brother watching the apartment. He still gets up every couple of hours to check the doors. Only one security camera caught something that night. Around four twenty-three, a man dressed in black runs across their backyard toward the main highway. Coty figures his car was hidden there, or someone was waiting for him.

I pause and look out the back window, not really focusing on anything. No one can get into Emily's back garden oasis here. It's completely fenced in and can only be accessed through the bakery. There's a prospect in the parking lot when Coty's not here.

Lily covers one of my hands with hers. "What is it?"

"There's been some things happening, even before the man showed up at my back door."

"Oh, my gosh, Lala." Emily places a hand over her heart. "That's scary. Have you told Coty?"

"Not outright." I shrug.

"What does that mean? And what's been happening?" Lily demands.

"One day this week, a postcard showed up. The only writing on it was my address, not even my name. It was stamped here in town. The front had a picture of the town on it, and the words, *Have a nice day*. I shrugged and threw it in the trash."

Lily locks eyes with Emily. "That is odd." Emily nods.

"It's not like the flower deliveries you got." I'm a little quick to defend the matter. "My situation isn't like yours."

"But what if it is?" Emily's question sends an eerie chill down my back.

"What else happened?" Lily lays her icing bag down and focuses on me.

"There've been a few times after work when I got into my car, I couldn't reach the gas pedal. I had to slide my seat forward."

"Keep going," Lily knows there's more.

"Well, when I got back home, my college coffee cup was in the sink. I don't remember using it. My favorite towel was hanging over the shower rod. I don't remember doing that. Maybe I really did just forget."

Lily lifts one eyebrow. Those things aren't too alarming, except for my seat being moved.

I keep going. "There was a new pack of beer in the fridge and six empty bottles in the trash."

"Let me guess. You don't remember that either?" Lily's mad or being sarcastic. I'm not sure which.

I shake my head. "And the blanket I keep on the couch was on the recliner. A few days ago, I went to the market. Dobbs went with me. Later, I found a *Mountain Dew* can on the floor on the passenger side. I figured it was Dobbs' and threw it away. Oh, and my gun was stolen from my nightstand. I know I put it back before I left."

"Okay. Some of that might be a coincidence, but I'm not buying it." Lily crosses her arms. She's definitely ticked off. "Either you call Coty and tell him, or I'm calling Jack."

"She's right. You need to tell Coty. I think you're being stalked." Emily's words hit me hard.

"Hey, Emily." Ava sticks her head in the door. "It's slowed down. Can Melody and I go to lunch now?"

"Yep. I'll take over. You girls go." Emily points at me. "Call Rodeo and keep icing cupcakes. Lily can help me out front if I need her."

"I need to run to the restroom. You good here for a few minutes?" Lily takes off her apron. I nod. "Take a little break and call Rodeo." She disappears down the short hallway.

"Sir, will you please stay on that side of the counter. It'll only take a few minutes to box your order up." Great. When it's just us three, Emily gets a rude customer. She goes quiet for a few minutes. "Sir, you can't come back here. Lily!"

Emily's scream is cut off just before there's a thud. The door flies open before I can move. Oh no.

"Got you." Trent rushes toward me.

How did he find me? Well, I guess it was no secret. He knew my hometown.

I scream and run toward the back door. It's a bad move. There's no way out of Emily's garden. Lily runs out of the restroom. Trent raises his arm with a gun in his hand. Lily freezes, and her eyes widen.

"No!" I scream and slam into him. The bullet goes into the ceiling. "Back inside." I shove Lily into the restroom. She can't get shot again.

Trent scrambles to his feet. Before he can lunge at me, Coty runs through the door and tackles him to the floor.

"Run, Lala!" Coty yells.

He needs help. I can't leave him. The restroom door opens, and Lily pulls me inside.

Coty

"My phone's on the counter. Please tell me you have yours in your pocket," Lily chokes back sobs.

From all the crashing sounds, Coty and Trent are destroying the kitchen.

"I told you this was a bad idea!" A deep voice, I don't recognize, yells.

"Let's get out of here," another man says.

"There are three of them." I frantically pull my phone from my pocket. Sirens pierce the air. I still make the call.

He answers on the first ring. "Kayla, tell me these cops aren't coming to the bakery."

"They are, Jack. Hurry." I end the call.

Sounds no longer come from the other side of the door. Whether they're gone or not, I have to know Coty's okay. I jerk the door open. Lily trembles, but follows close behind me. I spot his still body on the floor and lose it.

"Coty!" I fall to my knees next to him. He's too still. Blood runs from underneath his body.

"Emily," I cry to Lily. "Check on Emily."

Lily screams the moment she's through the door. Oh, please let Emily be okay.

The next few minutes are a blur. Cops rush in. Vikings pour through the doors against the cops' orders. Ambulances arrive and rush the four of us to the hospital. I try to ask questions, but the nurses won't tell me anything about Coty.

Minutes feel like hours as we wait. Lily and I are fine physically. Emily was knocked unconscious and has a concussion. She's being kept overnight for observation. Lily visited her. I stayed in the waiting room until Coty was brought to a room. I refuse to leave him.

Coty just got out of surgery. He was badly beaten. Some of his wounds were from objects around the kitchen. A few pierced his skin. He might as well have been stabbed. He wasn't shot, and the gun Trent had wasn't found. Coty has stitches in several places. The doctor told us how many and where they were. His parents listened to everything. It's all just a jumbled mess in my head. I can't process any of it.

I sit by his bed, lift his hand to my lips, and cry. "I'm so sorry," I whisper.

"Kayla," Jack says softly. I look up and meet his eyes. He's a strong man, but his eyes glisten. "Do you know who did this?"

"It was Trent. I didn't see the other two." I squeeze my eyes shut and cry harder. I've never wished harm on anyone. This changes things. I look back up at Coty's best friend. "Find him, Jack. Find him, and make him pay."

Jack doesn't say a word. He straightens, gives a firm nod, and storms from the room in a rage I never want coming for me. Jack McLeod is going for Trent Colby tonight, and he'll take an army of Vikings with him.

32
Jack

"Somebody give me something!" If we don't find Trent Colby soon, Jay's going to lose his reputation for being the most unhinged member of our family. "There's no way three men up and disappeared in this town."

"We're searching, Ghost," Hendrix assures me. Nick has us on a group call. "We want them, too."

"It would help if we knew what they were driving." Bankz is riding with Hendrix.

Jay sits next to me with his phone on speaker. "Nick, tell us you found something."

Nick found the vehicles registered to Trent Colby and Cory Coleman. He's been searching the store security cameras around town with no luck.

"Got him!" Nick exclaims. "Well, I'm almost positive I found him."

"Out with it, man. He's already got too much of a lead on us." I'm on the verge of losing my mind.

"A dark gray Ford Taurus passed Mel's not long after the attack happened. It's a rental with a Knoxville tag. I searched for rentals in Trent's name since Cory Coleman is still in jail and found nothing."

"Let me guess. The Taurus is in Coleman's name," Jay says.

"Yeah, that's on me, too, Jack. I should've thought of it." Nick's disappointed in himself. We'll deal with that later.

I turn around and drive towards Mel's. "This direction is toward the clubhouse, not Knoxville. Where would he go on this side of town?"

"Kayla's apartment is out here," Jay replies as we pass the gas stations. No Ford Taurus in the parking lot. No need to stop.

"Dobbs and I will check her apartment out," Parker offers.

"Jack, it might be a long shot, but Willow Park is out this way, too," Nick points out.

"Do you think Trent's connected to what happened to Matthew Rhodes?" Bankz asks.

"I'm not getting anything to connect them." Nick sighs. "But at this point, nothing would surprise me."

"Just rode by the apartments. Parker and Dobbs are there. No Taurus. Bankz and I will follow you to the river." Hendrix ends his side of the call.

I take the left toward Willow Park and press my foot hard on the gas pedal. This park is where I took Lily for our first unofficial date. It's where I first kissed her.

"Jack." Jay points to the entrance of the park. A black F-150 pulls out and heads in the opposite direction. "Nick said Adam Lang owns a black F-150."

I glance up at the fast-approaching car lights in the rearview mirror. Hendrix drives like a madman. I'm surprised he hasn't lost his license for speeding. I slow but still take the turn faster than I should, causing the tires to squeal.

"There he is." Jay's grin is pure evil. Trust me, my cousin isn't losing his reputation.

Jay scares me at times. He doesn't get to go after this one. Trent Colby is mine.

Trent spots us and runs for his car. I slam on the brakes, throw the truck into park, and cut him off before he gets inside. If he had, I would have broken the window to get him out.

"I…"

Nope. I slam my fist into his jaw hard enough to loosen some teeth. He doesn't get to speak. He almost killed my best friend. His ribs are next. They broke three of Coty's. The favor needs to be returned.

"You pointed a gun at my woman!" That one gets him beaten to the ground.

"Jack." Hendrix pounds on my back. I don't stop.

"Ghost!" A fist slams into my shoulder. I slowly turn my head toward my cousin. "Cops." Jay tackles me to the ground. Hendrix helps him hold my arms.

Four Sheriff cars fly into the parking lot and quickly surround us. I didn't hear the sirens until now. The Sheriff and six deputies get out with their guns raised.

"Jack McLeod." Sheriff Bowers stands in front of me, blocking my view of everything around us.

"He almost killed Coty." I don't wait for his questions.

"We know. An anonymous tip came in fifteen minutes ago. They said we'd find Trent Colby here." Nathan glances at Jay. "If you have a knife open, close it now."

"None open, Sheriff." Jay nods toward Trent. "We believe he was the man outside Kayla's apartment. He's her ex."

One of the deputies calls for an ambulance. Two more search the car. The others keep their guns out but not aimed at us.

"Sheriff!" Deputy Dean Johnson holds up a handgun with a pen.

"I bet money that's Kayla's stolen twenty-two," Jay says.

"I'm not betting with you, Jay." The Sheriff turns to me. "Due to how we found you, I have to take you to the station, Jack." He looks back at Jay. "I won't arrest him yet. Get your lawyer here quickly. She's smart enough to keep him out of a cell.

Jay starts to protest, but I shake my head. "It was worth it." And it was.

I don't fight or struggle in any way. I willingly let Sheriff Bowers put me in the back of his patrol car. I grin at my brothers as we drive away. No matter what happens to me, the man who hurt my friend and pointed a gun at my ole' lady got what was coming to him.

33
Kayla

It's been over twelve hours since the attack at the bakery. I've stayed by Coty's bedside the entire time except to go to the restroom. Thank goodness he's in a regular room with a small bathroom. He risked his life for me. I'll never forget that. No one has ever stood up for me before. Well, sometimes, I believe my brother tries. David brought me dinner earlier. He's the only member of my family who has shown up.

All of Coty's family has stopped by, his real family and his club brothers. Ember took Mary home when visiting hours were over. His parents take turns staying a few hours at a time. It was nice seeing his grandparents, just not for this reason. I should have gone to the ranch several times to visit them. It's my fault that there's distance between us. I put it there. My mad against the world campaign burned a lot of bridges. Hopefully, I'm on the road to rebuilding them.

Just before two in the morning, Coty stirs. I quickly stand. Leaning over him, with a trembling hand, I bring his to my lips. He's finally waking up.

"Coty." I release a shaky breath. I hate myself for being so mean to him.

He takes a deep breath as his eyes blink open. "Hey, Sparky. You okay?"

I lightly laugh. "I should be asking you that."

"Hospital?" He sounds so tired.

"Yeah."

"How bad?"

I don't want to tell him, but he deserves to know. "Well, you have three broken ribs. Some of the objects they hit you with from the kitchen cut you. You have stitches on both arms and your back." I choke back a sob. "They cracked your skull."

He reaches up and wipes a tear from my cheek with his thumb. "Don't cry. I'm here."

"I was so scared." I kiss the back of his hand again.

"I was scared I wouldn't get there in time."

"I'm sorry. This is my fault."

"Hey, no. You're not responsible for what other people do."

He's sweet for saying that, but Trent was here because of me. My fault, plain and simple.

He shifts slightly and groans. "I'm not looking good in the macho department and saving my girl."

He can tease all he wants. I'm not playing along with it. "There were three of them, Coty. You're alive. That's all that matters."

"Three? I saw a second man. Do you know who Trent's buddies were?"

I shake my head. "I didn't see them, and I didn't recognize their voices."

"They get him?"

This, I'm proud to tell him. "Yeah, but Jack got him first."

He lightly chuckles and groans again. "*He* alive?"

"He was brought in unconscious. Sheriff Bowers had him moved to another hospital. They won't tell us where, though." It's for the best. I know a few Vikings who would barge in after Trent if they knew where he was.

He lays his palm against my cheek. "It's going to be okay, Sparky. Promise."

"I'm so sorry, Coty. So, so sorry. For everything. I've been a royal B to you since you've been back." I have, and it was wrong.

"We're past it now, but I'm guessing Trent has something to do with that."

I nod. "I blamed you for my bad choices. You left. You weren't here."

"What did Trent do to you, Lala?"

"Things I don't want to remember," I whisper.

What did Trent Colby do? I'm not ready to dive into all of it. A lot can happen in three months, especially when you're in the wrong place. Coty's hurt. He needs to rest. Still, he deserves to know something. For now, I'll make it as short as possible and tell him about the last time I saw Trent. We can talk about the details when he's out of here.

The last time I was with Trent Colby was the week between Christmas and New Year's two years ago. We were kind of dating for three months. I can't really call it dating because I didn't want to be there. I stayed out of fear.

I met Trent at a party Kira took me to. Everybody was drinking, including me. Trent, Kira, and several others were snorting lines of Coke. A few people had needles. Another girl fought back when one of Trent's friends got a little too handsy. She was slapped across the face a couple of times and shoved out the door. I later learned that Corine Whitmore found a taxi and made it back to her dorm. The following week, her parents transferred her to a college near her hometown in Alabama.

I got trapped in a room with Trent that night. He was drunk, high, or both. I stopped drinking hours before. I didn't know at the time what happened to Corine after she was shoved outside. I was scared, trapped, and felt like I had no choice. I let it happen, and he kept coming after me every day after that.

Trent took me to a low-rated hotel near Myrtle Beach, South Carolina. He called it a surprise holiday vacation. The entire trip was horrible.

"Can we go home now?" Asking was pointless, but I did it anyway.

"No!" Trent snaps. "I already told you. We're meeting my friends. It's important."

"Can't they come to Tennessee to see you?"

He pushes me against the wall. "No. The plan was to meet here. You're stupid. Always have been. Don't know why I put up with an ignorant woman like you," he mumbles the last part.

I'm used to him calling me stupid and other names. The plan? That's different, and doesn't sound good.

Trent eases up to me and grabs the hem of my shirt. "I know what we can do to pass the time."

He leans in to kiss me. Ew. I jerk away, ripping my shirt. I need to get out of here before his friends show up.

Grabbing my purse, I rush to the door. "I'm going to the vending machines for drinks and snacks."

"Get back here!" Thankfully, Trent's phone rings. His plan is more important than stopping me. He takes the call as I hurry out the door.

I have nowhere to go and no plan. The vending machines are the last thing on my mind. I hurry into the row of trees next to the hotel and hide. I need to figure out how to get home. My phone dings.

Trent: *Get back here!*
Me: *No.*
Trent: *Now, Kayla, or you'll regret it.*
Me: *No. We're done. I never want to see you again.*

Let's just say the string of curse words and horrible names he called me are some I never want to hear again.

Trent: *I'll find you. You'll pay for this. You can't hide from me.*

Less than ten minutes later, a car pulls into the parking lot and parks next to Trent's car. Two men get out and knock on the door to our room. Trent happily lets them in. Why I'm still watching, I don't know. Another ten minutes and the parking lot fills with police cars. I smile when Trent's brought out in handcuffs. A drug bust. He's going away for a while. I'm finally free of him.

I was too afraid to move until after the cops left. I walked about three miles to a Walmart. I grabbed a soda and a prepackaged sandwich from the deli. The cashier directed me to the bus station. It was a mile away.

I purchased a ticket to Nashville. My brother picked me up from there. I secretly stayed a few days with David.

I went to the Viking Den that weekend. Coty and Jack weren't back yet. No one knew if they'd return anytime soon. A club bunny, Missy, happily talked about her night with Rodeo before he left. It was disgusting. It's where my anger and hate for Coty started, and I built on it every day since.

"I'm sorry, Lala. You didn't deserve for any of that to happen to you." Coty listened to me without interrupting. "If I had known there was a chance for us, I probably would have talked Jack into coming back sooner."

"Why did you two stay out there so long?"

"My best friend was drowning here in grief for his sister and the pain of his family. Every day, out there, he let go a little more and became close to the Jack he used to be. I couldn't take that from him. So, I followed his lead."

That makes sense. It's something Coty would do for a friend. It makes him a better man than any that I know.

"I made one bad decision after another and blamed you for them, and you were out there being a true friend. I'm the one who's sorry."

"Well, we can't change it, but we can both heal from it."

"You really think we can?" It would be a dream come true for me.

"I know we can, Sparky. I'm not letting you go. I won't trap you or force you to be with me. I'll hold onto you with love."

"I love you, Coty." I wipe the tears from my cheek. Of course, his sweet talk makes me cry.

"I love you, too, Sparky." He motions with his finger for me to come closer. "Now, kiss me, and let's seal this promise."

A promise sealed with a kiss. Absolutely. I lean down and gently press my lips to his.

Epilogue
Coty

My first Valentine's Day with Lala isn't going how I'd hoped. I've never planned anything on Valentine's Day before. I wanted to do something special for her tonight.

Surprisingly, she didn't throw a fit when I asked her to work at the Den tonight instead of the Roadhouse. I've sat at the table closest to the door for church all night with her in my sight. It's not like I can do much else anyway. I could, but getting up would have a slew of people on my head.

My parents are here tonight. Ember and Maci are helping Lala bartend. Not sure how I feel about my sister behind a bar. Jack has loudly stated his disapproval of his sister bartending. Maci simply smiles and keeps serving drinks. My youngest sister, Mary, is up at the main house with Everly. Her older brother, Logan, is watching over them tonight. The girl he liked blew him off tonight. Logan's mad at the world right now. He's the perfect Viking to watch over his sister and mine. He's not a patched member, but we all know he will be someday.

I was released from the hospital this morning. Four nights there were more than enough for me. I believe Lala and Lily conspired with the hospital staff to keep me there an extra day or two.

"How's the ribs?" Jack sits down next to me. Thankfully, Ciara Hollis kept him from being put in a cell. It's still unclear whether he'll be charged. Miss Hollis will fight for just probation if it happens.

"Sore." I could lie, but he'd see through me.

Mack nods to Jack and moves to stand in front of the doors to church. Worley stands behind him.

Jack glances at Lala and back at me. "You ready?"

My eyes drop to the cut draped over Worley's left arm. "I never told her. She's gonna be pissed."

"That's why it's better to do it while you're wounded and recovering." Jack nods to his dad, and on cue, the music stops.

"Vikings!" Mack yells over the crowd. Everyone quietens down and gives our Prez their attention. "Lala, you wanna join us?" He motions her over.

She narrows her eyes and looks around the room. When she doesn't move, Lily takes her hand and leads her through the kitchen to the common room. She nervously walks over to stand behind me.

"The patched members already know. Now, it's time to make it official. A couple of weeks ago, Coty Michaels claimed Kayla Chambers as his ole' lady."

Lala quickly moves in front of me. I'm still not allowed out of this chair—her orders, not the doctor's.

"You did what?"

"I claimed you." I nod to my brothers behind her. "They agreed."

"Two weeks, and you haven't told me?"

"Well," I run a hand through my hair. "I've kinda been busy lately." It's a lame excuse, but also true.

Worley hands me her property of cut. I turn it around to show her the Viking Warriors emblem Nanny designed in memory of Ariel. I point to my road name, Rodeo, on the bottom rocker. I flip it around and show her the patch with Lala on it.

Sitting up as straight as I can, I hold the cut open. "Come on, Sparky. You know you want this."

Her eyes drop to the cut and back to mine. "Are you sure?"

"I've told you at least a hundred times this week that I love you. Yeah, I'm sure."

She lowers and slides her arms through the sleeves. Mindful of my ribs and stitches on my arms and back, she leans down and wraps her arms around my neck.

"I love you, too, Coty," she whispers.

"Vikings!" Mack shouts. "Raise your glass and celebrate Rodeo and Lala! She now has the protection and rights as an ole' lady."

The room erupts in shouts and cheers. When Lala tries to stand up straight, I pull her onto my lap.

"Coty, no. You'll hurt yourself."

"I'm not *that* hurt." She knows it as well as I do. "We need to talk about some things."

"We do," she agrees. "But we can do that later tonight. I need to get back."

"Nope. Parker's here." I point to the bar. Ember and Maci have all the help they need.

"Okay. What's so urgent it can't wait?"

"I don't want to stay in your apartment. I can't go there." I now understand how Jack feels about returning to his house.

"Why? Trent's in jail. He's not getting out for a long time."

She finally opened up and told me about her relationship with Trent. If he weren't in jail, I'd hunt him down and give him twice the beating Jack did.

And it's true. Trent Colby survived the beating Jack gave him. He's been charged with three counts of assault and battery. Emily Powell is still shaken up, but medically, she's okay. Skip was knocked unconscious with a blunt object in the parking lot. He complains of headaches, but otherwise he's okay, too. Trent won't name the two men who helped him, and I didn't get a good look at them before I was knocked out. We're sure Willis Sanford and Adam Lang were his accomplices. Since we can't prove it, the cops aren't taking it seriously.

I close my eyes. "I can't go there, Sparky. Please don't ask me to."

"Well, I don't want to stay in your room here."

I don't either. "I'm not asking you to. I have something better in mind."

"Oh?" Now, she's intrigued.

"Yeah. Since I now officially have an ole' lady, I kinda need a job," I tease.

"A job? Where?"

"My grandfather needs help on the ranch. The position comes with a two-bedroom cabin." I gently slide my thumb across her cheek.

"Are you really sure this is what you want? I'm what you want? I mean, you got hurt because of me, and badly."

"I finally got you. Even before I had you, I would have died for you."

Her mouth falls open with a gasp.

"You've lost your mind. I love you, but your mind is so warped."

"Sparky, the only thing on my mind is you, me, and a couple of kids." Her eyes widen. "Someday," I add.

"Someday," she repeats softly.

I cup her cheek in my palm. "So, say yes, Sparky, and kiss me."

"Yes," she whispers just before her lips press against mine.

Fighting for the Innocent

Thank you for reading Coty – Viking Warriors MC - Book 2.

This book and series carry a hidden meaning. Some of you may know, most don't. On January 18, 2011, we lost my daughter, Kacy Magnolia Roberson, and her unborn daughter, Angel Magnolia Roberson. There are also things from life in this book. Some of the things Kayla went through, so have I.

People have asked me for years to write a book about Kacy's story. They said I could help so many people. A few of those people were genuine in that request. Most, I fear, only wanted a play-by-play of what happened to her. I'll never write that. But I do want to tell parts of Kacy's story. I'm not sure if it'll help anyone. When I decided to write an MC series, I thought I could share bits and pieces of Kacy's story here. I'll never share it all. I can't. Writing this book ripped me open so many times. Seriously, my friends even called to check on me. It was hard.

In this series, Ariel's story is Kacy's story. Everything about Ariel's story is real. Some of the other scenes are, too. Everything else in the series may be different and changed; just know Ariel's part won't. It's as close as I could get to sharing it.

If you or someone you know is in an abusive relationship, I encourage you to leave. Nothing is more important than your life. It doesn't get better. It only gets worse. Sometimes, like with Kacy, there are no warning signs. Sometimes, it only happens once. We didn't have the warning signs.

If you need help, here's a place to start:
National Domestic Violence Hotline
CALL 1-800-799-SAFE (7233)
CHAT www.thehotline.org
TEXT "START" to 88788

And for love is respect for youth, focusing on healthy dating relationships:
CALL 1-866-331-9474
CHAT www.loveisrespect.org
TEXT "LOVEIS" to 22522

Follow Me

Sign up for my Newsletter:
https://linktr.ee/debbiehydeauthor

Facebook Page:
Debbie Hyde Author

Facebook Groups:
Debbie Hyde's Reader Group: This one is for all of my books. I hold giveaways in the group.
Debbie Hyde's Book Launch Team: I would love to have you on my book launch team! The team gets all my book news first. They get to participate in the writing process with me at times and even help with cover design ideas. Team members get first chance at Beta & ARC opportunities. Join me today!
For the Love of a Shaw: This group is dedicated to the series.
Hayden Falls series: This group is dedicated to the series.
The Dawson Boys series: This group is dedicated to the series.

The Fireside Book Café – This is a book community group with various Authors and books from every genre. We hold Giveaways here, too.

Instagram:
www.instagram.com/debbie_hyde_author

Twitter:
Debbie Hyde5

Acknowledgments

When I decided to release book 1 in this series on January 18th, an amazing tribe of women stepped up to help keep me encouraged and writing. Without them, I wouldn't have made it.

Nancie Blume, thank you so much for all you do for me, and not just in my author career. You've been my Alpha Reader long before we knew what it was called. This is my 22nd novel, and you've been there for every one of them. You kept me on track with this one. You knew when scenes were hard and personal, and that I wasn't okay. You called and messaged me every day and night. There were some really long nights, too. Thank you for the information you're giving about motorcycle clubs. I'm going to stop here because I could write a whole chapter for you. I love you, lil buddy.
HAPPY BIRTHDAY, LIL BUDDY!

Wendy Sizemore, thank you so much for being my friend and unbiological sister. You prefer the books when they're finished because you love getting the whole story at once. Thank you for all the calls and texts helping me come up with story ideas. You always read between the lines lol. Some of my books wouldn't be what they are without you. This past week, you messaged and asked if I was okay. You didn't know I just wrote a hard chapter and was broken. I replied, no. You called right away. I love you, Winnie.

To my beyond awesome Beta Readers, Victoria Trout, Tiffany Buras Parker, Nancie Blume, and Chrystal Harman. You ladies are beyond amazing. You had less than a day to do this, and you came through brilliantly. I wouldn't have made the pre-order deadline without you. We had 11 minutes to spare.

To my amazing Admins and Mods of The Fireside Book Café group, thank you so so much for keeping the group going through the two medical issues my family had and while I buckled down and finished this book. I don't know everything you ladies did to pull it off, but thank you. We are definitely a tribe.

Thank you, Victoria Trout/Heidi Swift. I'm so grateful I met you. You have become family to me. I think we agreed on cousins. I think it's more. You have been so supportive through this book. Your messages and encouragement kept me going. I wish we didn't live in separate states.

Tiffany Buras Parker, thank you so much for being there when I need you. We don't get to talk every day, but girl, you know how to show up right on time. You're one of the best beta readers I could ever hope for. This book wouldn't have made it without your help. I'm so glad we got to meet at the Fair. I hope we can do more events together. I love your books. I can't wait to read your next one. Your shifter series is my favorite. And then there's always Sam. I love Sam.

To Ghostface_gulfcoast, thank you for being our Jack. I'm glad I found you on Instagram. Thank you so much for helping Indie authors. I don't think you get enough credit or thank yous for all you do. And thank you for the sacrifices you make for our country. We'll have you back when it's Jay's turn to share his story.

Thank you to Coty Pearson for being the cover model for Coty. Thank you for the motorcycle club information you give me. I had no idea where to start with this. I'd look stupid without you, lol.

Thank you to Donya Claxton for doing Coty's photo shoot. It was awesome. You're photos are beautiful. Can't wait to see you at the Fair this year.

Thank you, Darin Worley. Hey, cuz. Thank you for being our Worley Bird in this series, and real life lol. You were the first person I contacted when I decided to write an MC series. Hope my guys don't step on too many toes for you.

To Frank Thompson. Dude, you are so so missed. There was no way I could write an MC series and not have Cloudy Daze in there. Fly high my friend.

Big Papa, aka, Jerry Blume. Thanks dude for allowing me to keep your wife on the phone and text messages all the time. Thank you for being in my series. We can't have Lil Mama in here without you. You're also a bartender in the *For the Love of a Shaw* series. Take care of my best friend, dude.

To Joe Milam, thank you for talking to me in a Walmart parking lot in middle Tennessee. I hope you see this. I gave you a character and helped you out with a road name. Hopefully, we'll meet again sometime. Meeting you on New Year's Day gave me a new purpose. I drove away, hearing in my head, *Meet them all.* Now, I'm on a mission to meet as many bikers as I can. In fact, I'm getting a journal and hoping they'll sign it. I'm saving the first spot for you.

To Chrystal Harman, the BEST PA and Sissi I could ever hope for, want, and need. Thank you for all you do for my books, but I thank you more for becoming part of my found family. We met through T. L. Drake when I found her book *Wren* from the *Road Demons* series in a contest and tagged her. Y'all didn't know it was there. We helped her win that! Over the next couple of years, you became more than a friend. We have so much in common it was scary. Thank you for becoming my PA last year. Three years, Sissi, and eternity to go. You can't get rid of me. For this book and series, you gave me the name Lily for our female lead. You gave me Willow Creek for the town. You gave me Shepherd as an Enforcer. He's in the Texas chapter. Thank you, girl, for everything. Mainly for listening when I needed you.

The Dawson Boys

Holding Her ~ Book One
Harrison & Tru
   Losing her destroyed me. One letter gave me hope. Like a man on a mission, I went after her.

I Do It For You ~ Book Two
Bryan & Dana
   Sometimes, slow, steady, and sweet are not the best way to go. Did I wait too long? Did my plan fail? I don't know, but I'd do anything for her.

Everything I Ever Wanted ~ Book Three
Calen & Daisy
   "Get out!" I've shouted those words every day. Does she listen? Not a chance. She challenges me. She tests me. How did she become everything I ever wanted?

Book Four ~ Coming Soon!

Hayden Falls

Forever Mine ~ Book One
Aiden and E
 Today, I'm going home to a town that wrote me off years ago. Home to a job I never planned on taking. Home to watch the woman I love marry someone else. I'm not going to survive this.

Only With You ~ Book Two
Miles and Katie
 My career is strong and sure. My personal life is a mess. My only regret is keeping her a secret. Winning her back won't be easy, but I have to try.

Giving Her My Heart ~ Book Three
Jasper and Hannah
 The dance teacher annoys me at every turn until she twirls her way into my heart and my daughter's. Now, I need to find a way to get her to stay.

Finding Home ~ Book Four
Luke and Riley
 I was the fun brother until my twin almost died in a fire. Now, I'm a mess. Then she comes along. I'm charming, but am I enough for her to stay?

Listening to My Heart ~ Book Five
Phillip and Tara
 My family took the biggest part of my heart from me. A piece I didn't know existed. After nine years, the woman who holds every piece of my heart returns, bringing a huge secret with her. This time, no one will keep me from her.

A Hayden Falls Christmas
Spend Christmas in Hayden Falls. Enjoy short stories of the five couples we've met so far, plus two of the town's beloved families.

Falling for You ~ Book Six
Lucas and Hadley
I'm a career-minded deputy. I wasn't looking for love. Until my little brother butted into my love life, I never even noticed the woman right in front of me.

Finally Home ~ Book Seven
Aaron and Kennedy
If I had known joining the Army would have cost me her, I never would have enlisted.

Protecting You ~ Book Eight
Leo and Kyleigh
I'm the quiet brother. Nothing gets under my skin. Well, not until a little brunette swings her way into my life and changes everything.

A Hayden Falls Christmas ~ Two
Spend Christmas in Hayden Falls. Enjoy short stories of the three couples we've met since last Christmas, plus updates on a few of the town's beloved families. Oh, there are lots of surprises this season.

Book Nine ~ Coming Soon!

For the Love of a Shaw

When A Knight Falls ~ Book One
Gavin & Abby
The future Earl will battle his long-time enemy more than once when he falls for his nursemaid. Will Abby marry the wrong man to save an innocent girl?

Falling for the Enemy ~ Book Two
Nate & Olivia
Nathaniel Shaw takes a job to prove his worth to his father. He loses his heart to the mysterious woman in his crew, only to discover she isn't who she claims to be.

A Knight's Destiny ~ Book Three
Nick & Elizabeth
Nicholas Shaw is a Knight without a title, but he's loved the Duke's sister for years. When Elizabeth needs protection and runs away, Nick goes with her rather than sending her to her brother.

Capturing A Knight's Heart ~ Book Four
Jax & Nancie
The rules of society don't bind Jackson Shaw. He's free to roam as he pleases until he stumbles across a well-kept secret of Miss Nancie's. Will Nancie guard her heart and push him away? Or has she truly captured this Knight's heart?

A Duke's Treasure ~ Book Five
Sam & Dani
The Duke of Greyham, Samuel Dawson, has loved Lady Danielle Shaw for years. Dani stumbles into his darkest secret, leaving Sam no choice but to steal her away.

A Knight's Passion ~ Book Six
Caleb & Briley
Caleb Shaw feels lost, alone, and misunderstood. His mind is haunted by his past. While running for his life, he devises a plan to save Briley. The bluff is called, trapping them together forever.

A Mysterious Knight ~ Book Seven
Alex & Emily
Alexander Shaw had no light, peace, or love if he didn't have her. The day she sent him away almost destroyed him. Emily's trapped in her father's secrets and can't break free no matter how much she wants to. Alex will risk his life to free hers.

About the Author

Debbie Hyde is a Contemporary & Historical Romance Author. Her series include, at this time, For the Love of a Shaw, The Dawson Boys, Hayden Falls, and Viking Warriors MC. More series are planned. Another will be released in 2025.

Debbie loves helping readers, authors, and narrators connect. She created the Facebook group, The Fireside Book Café, for that purpose.

She's a seamstress and a cake decorator. When she's not reading and writing, or running around for her children and grandchildren, they keep her VERY busy, she loves creating book covers and graphics.

Debbie Hyde

www.ingramcontent.com/pod-product-compliance
Lightning Source LLC
LaVergne TN
LVHW041705060526
838201LV00043B/580